Her Safe Harbor

Crawford Family 4

HOLLY BUSH

Chapter One

Boston, 1893

"WHAT DO YOU MEAN YOU are planning to travel again? You have just returned," Jane Crawford said to her daughter. "No more traveling. Mr. Rothchild won't like it. Will you, Jeffrey?"

Jennifer Crawford watched as her mother leaned forward from her place at the table in the family dining room at Willow Tree to cover Jeffrey's hand with her own, purse her lips, and wink at him. It made Jennifer ill to think that if she were to spend her life with Jeffrey, as he and her mother had already planned, she would be subject to her mother's ridiculous flirting and fawning over her husband, and in turn his obsequious and affected gratitude and flattery toward her mother.

"Jolene has asked me to come and help her in her new home in Washington when Max takes his seat in the U.S. Senate. She will be very busy, and Melinda will need attention. I have already told her I will come," Jennifer said.

Jeffrey took a sip of his wine and looked at her over the rim of the cut crystal glass. "The Morgans are expecting us at their gala. I'm sure you don't want to disappoint them."

"I do not," she said. "But you will have to make my excuses. Certainly, they understand what a momentous occasion this is for our family."

"There is nothing momentous about the occasion at all! This person your sister has married is nothing! His family barely touches any good Boston society. And anyway, politicians are inevitably lowborn and crass," Jane declared. "He is nothing to us and your sisters are dead to me."

"Jane," her father, William Crawford, said to his wife in a plaintive voice Jennifer was accustomed to hearing.

"It is true!" Jane said. "After everything I have done for Jolene and Julia? For them to turn their backs on their own mother?"

"Mother, please. Mr. Rothchild does not want to hear any of this."

Jane demurred with a shrug. "He is *nearly* family."

Jennifer continued to eat, staring down at her plate so she did not have to view her mother's smug smile. When she looked up, Jeffrey's eyes were on her.

"I have already replied to the Morgans for both of us," he said.

"I'm sure they will not miss one lone person from the hundreds they invite."

"This is business, Jennifer," he said. "They are longtime customers of the bank, and if not for Harry Morgan's introductions we would have missed out on having some very important clients. I'm sure you understand that."

"Wouldn't having a family member who is a U.S. senator be good for gaining new clients?" she asked.

Her mother *harrumphed.*

"Jennifer," Jeffrey admonished. "It has already been decided. We are going to the Morgans'."

Jeffrey's lips were a hard line, and his eyes cold as he spoke. She recognized that look and didn't challenge him or say more. In fact, no one at the table conversed, and she was feeling embarrassed by the set-down. She continued to eat and sipped her wine, willing herself to be patient until it was time to make her escape to her rooms. But what would she do if they were married? How would she escape him?

Dessert had just been served when her father cleared his throat, and every head turned to him. "If Jolene has asked for your help, then you should attend her. I will make your excuses to Harry Morgan."

Jennifer was shocked and stared at her father, not daring to witness Jeffrey's or her mother's reaction, as her father rarely exerted himself on her or her sisters' behalf. Jennifer didn't believe he didn't care, in fact, she felt he cared very deeply about all of them, and was mortally depressed when Jillian went to live with Julia. But he'd always stayed clear of the family machinations, believing that was his wife's purview, Jennifer thought. And, if truth be told, she felt Julia was correct when she said in her letters that Father wanted to avoid the living hell that his wife would make of his life if he interfered. She also thought that her father was a bit frightened of Jane and her moods and maneuvers, just like everyone else in the household.

Jeffrey waved away the servant offering him a cordial. "I'm sorry I'll be unable to stay longer this evening. There is somewhere I must be."

"I'm so sorry, Jeffrey," her mother said. "Must you go now before we adjourn to the music room?"

A servant hurried forward to pull back Jeffrey's chair as he stood. "It is rarely wise to put off an important task, especially as current circumstances are not as friendly as I would like," he said, and stared at Jennifer.

"Escort Mr. Rothchild to the door, Jennifer. It is the least you can do," her mother said.

Jennifer walked beside him down the long hallway of Willow Tree, the sound of her slippers tapping on the marble floors breaking the silence. She watched Jeffrey as Bellings came from his position at the door to help him on with his coat and hand him his top hat and walking cane. Jeffrey was tall—taller than her by a good number of inches, and she was a tall woman. He had a handsome face, but his eyes never matched any gaiety he showed with laughter or smiles; in fact, his dark eyes were disconcerting. Frightening even, on some occasions. She'd thought him very attractive when she first met him, but with each encounter, mostly arranged by her mother, she'd felt a cold chill pass across her shoulders when he spoke to her in the way he had at the dinner table. Let alone when . . . well, she would not think of that.

Jeffrey glared at Bellings and the servant retreated toward the grand staircase that wrapped around the edge of the foyer. Jeffrey turned his stare on her.

"Do you believe I enjoy being contradicted by my future wife in front of her parents?"

Jennifer swallowed. "I did not mean to contradict you."

"However, you did. I would have expected you to have more respect for your betrothed as I do for your mother and father."

"I do appreciate how kind you are to my family. Especially to my mother," she said purposefully and looked at him.

Jeffrey tapped his cane on the floor. "She is dreadful to you. I won't allow her interference after our marriage. She is an altogether unpleasant woman in my estimation."

Jennifer felt her heart skip a beat as he defended her and promised her protection, but she wondered if she would be exchanging one unpleasant master for another.

"I am most surprised your father chose to interfere between you and me." Jeffrey leaned forward and spoke softly. "Let me be very clear. I will expect complete loyalty in a wife."

Then, as if for Bellings's benefit, he pulled her hands to his lips for a kiss and stared into her eyes with intensity and passion, speaking loudly enough that the servant would hear. "I will count the days until I see you again, my dear."

Jeffrey went out the door and Jennifer drew a deep breath and turned, intending to go to her rooms. Jane stood at the bottom of the staircase. She dismissed Bellings.

"How clumsy you are, Jennifer. Pitting your father against your fiancé over something as inconsequential as Jolene's imagined needs. You will stay here and you will attend the Morgan gala. I will not see you squander this opportunity that I have made available to you from the goodness of my heart."

"He is not my fiancé. I have never said yes to his proposal and may never do so."

"You are ridiculous! Your engagement has been discussed at parties and in boardrooms. Do not pretend to threaten me. I will not stand for it."

Jennifer thought about her sister Jolene's offer to have Jennifer live with them indefinitely in Washington.

Perhaps that thought was enough to give her the courage necessary to be clear to her mother. "I have not accepted his proposal, Mother. I do not care what Boston society thinks of me so it will make little difference to me what is said. You had best be very careful who you announce this to, as you alone will be embarrassed in the end." Jennifer turned and climbed the steps as her mother bellowed from the foyer.

"You are the one who took one look at Jeffrey Rothchild, had one dance with him, and promoted him in such a way that he was hired at the Crawford Bank by your father. Do not pretend now that you want nothing to do with him after you have pursued him. Your father hired him to please you, thinking to begin to prepare his soon to be son-in-law. Don't pretend now that he is nothing to you!"

Jennifer's hands were shaking as she approached her room. She could still hear her mother shouting below her. He maid, Eliza, opened her door.

"Good evening, miss," Eliza said.

"Help me out of this corset. I will not be going downstairs any more this evening."

"Yes, miss."

"Please unhook it. I cannot breathe. And the necklace. Remove my necklace. Quickly!"

Jennifer dropped down onto the chair in front of her vanity where Eliza had guided her. She could feel her heart pounding in her chest and hear its beat in her ears. She fumbled with the clasp of her bracelet and could not open it. She tried to pull it off over her hand, digging the gems and metalwork into her skin. Eliza stilled her hands with her own and worked the clasp until the bracelet slipped off.

"There, miss, it is off," Eliza said. "Take slow breaths. I will have a tray sent up. A nice steamy cup of tea will be just the thing."

Eliza pulled Jennifer's dress over her head, undid her corset, and led her to the screen in her room. She handed her a dressing gown of thick fabric and Jennifer pulled it on over her silk chemise and drawers. Her fingers shook as she knotted the belt, and she took long, even breaths to calm the heartbeat that she could still hear in her ears. She came out from behind the screen as Eliza stoked the fire in her room.

"Your tray is on the way, and I've asked Cook to send some of those delicious wafers she's been making with the icing that is so sweet. I had two myself this morning. And did I tell you about the new man working in the stables and garages? Oh my," she said.

Jennifer relaxed listening to the lilt of Eliza's voice and the rhythm of her words telling stories about the staff belowstairs. She was seated at her dressing table now and sipping tea while Eliza unpinned her hair and brushed it until the curls were shining. Jennifer closed her eyes and laid her hand on Eliza's.

"Thank you," she said. "I am fine now."

"Of course you are," Eliza said briskly. "Have you had any word about how your sister is faring in the Capital?"

"She has written again to ask me to live with them permanently."

"Has your answer changed, miss?"

"No. It has not. Although I will travel there soon for my brother-in-law's swearing in. I'd like you to come with me, Eliza. We will stay for two weeks or more."

"Yes, miss. Do you know—"

Jennifer and Eliza both turned as they heard shouting from the hallway. Eliza hurried to the door and opened it a few inches to peer outside the room.

"Is that Mother shouting?" Jennifer asked.

Eliza nodded. "It is."

Jennifer went to the door and listened from within her room. She could hear her father begging for restraint and her mother shouting back. It was about her, she knew, and no doubt, her father was bearing the brunt of his defense of her at the dinner table against Jeffrey. She pulled open the door.

"Mother!" she said as she walked to her parents where they stood at the end of the massive hallway where the family quarters were. "The servants will hear you. Please."

"I will not be made a fool of by you or anyone else in this family. I will not!" Jane shouted, and suddenly bent over at the waist in obvious pain.

"Jane?" her father said with concern, and took his wife's elbow. "Are you unwell? Shall I call the doctor?"

"Get me to my rooms, William," a white-faced Jane said. "Call for Mildred."

"I think you should see a doctor," he said. "This is the second time . . ."

"I will not be badgered!" she said, and then faltered farther into her husband's arms.

"Fetch Mildred," Jennifer said to Eliza, and then turned to her mother. "I will help you change and get settled."

Her mother shook her head. "I want nothing to do with you. Where is Mildred? William! Get me to my rooms!"

Jennifer folded her hands at her waist and watched as her father helped her mother down the hallway. Mildred hurried by, giving instructions to a young woman for what was to be brought to her mistress's room. She eyed Jennifer with barely concealed contempt.

* * *

"How is Mother this morning?" Jennifer asked her father as they rode in the family carriage into the heart of Boston the following day.

"I do not know. She would not allow me into her rooms and Mildred had nothing to say."

"Nothing to say or wouldn't say?"

Her father smiled at her just as if she'd never asked the question. "What are your plans for today, Jennifer? If you're not too busy, I have another packet for you."

She nodded. "Of course. Send Wickers with the details."

The carriage rolled to a stop at a discreet side door on the massive stone building that was the Crawford Bank, and her father stepped out. "Take Miss Crawford to the lobby."

Jennifer pulled her gloves tight as they rounded the corner and then accepted the doorman's help down the two carriage steps. She drew herself up as she'd seen Jolene and her mother do on so many occasions, straightening her back, and slowly turning her head from side to side. Gentlemen stopped on either side of the dark carpet that went the entire way to the bank's marble foundation.

The doorman nodded and opened the door for her to enter. "Good morning, Miss Crawford."

Snow had begun to swirl around her, sprinkling white on her dark blue walking coat and velvet hat, the pheasant feather dipping with each step. The men who had stopped to let her pass were tipping their hats or removing them.

"Good morning, McAtee! It is a lovely morning, even with this wretched snow."

"Let me hold my umbrella over you so you don't get wet," a young man shouted, and received laughter in reply from the men around him.

"Thank you, but I'm almost inside," she said, and tossed her dark blond curls over her shoulder as she smiled brightly at the man holding his umbrella out to her like an offering.

Jennifer entered the bank with a nod to the doorman.

"She smiled at you, boyo," another man said to the man holding the umbrella. "Lucky dog, you."

"She did," he replied, still staring at the now closed bank door. "She did."

"I time my mornings to be just here when she arrives," the man said. "'Twas a dreadful stretch when she was away. I thought I'd right died when she come back."

* * *

"I'll take your wrap, miss," O'Brien said.

"Thank you," Jennifer replied to the young red-haired woman her father had assigned to her as a companion while she was at the bank. He could hardly have designated a secretary, since he would not have liked having a man so close to her and the secretary most certainly would not like working for or with a woman. So a compromise was reached for when Jennifer was at the bank, ostensively as a bright, lovely decoration meant to greet and converse with important customers of her family's bank.

"Who is scheduled for today, O'Brien?" she asked when she was seated behind the desk in the small anteroom off of the parlor lobby, as it was known. A private side entrance for important customers, near the one her father had entered, led directly to this room. Jennifer would serve tea and coffee and inquire after the customer's and his family's health, much like any lady would do when entertaining in her own home, before her father or one of her father's employees took the customer to their office.

Jennifer knew that her sister Jolene had done her share of this sort of thing during the time she was married, while her first husband, Turner, worked just two floors above, near his father-in-law's offices. Her father was not enamored of the idea of her continuing on with what Jolene had started, however, as she was unmarried. Jennifer argued that O'Brien was always with her and that her assistant was the daughter of Thomas O'Brien, who managed their family stables, whom her father had known since his youth, when the then young, fabled horseman from Ireland had landed in the States, and whom he had trusted and employed for all of their adult lives. But her father was won over when Jennifer confessed she could not abide being at Willow Tree for days on end with only Jane Crawford as a companion.

"Just a Mr. Carter, Miss Crawford," O'Brien replied as she glanced at the list she held in her hand. "Your sister's notes indicate he had a sickly child the last time he was here, almost three years ago. But I cannot tell if the child was sick with a passing fever or cold or sickly with some long-term ailment."

"I will have to see how the conversation goes," Jennifer said. "What other information did Jolene leave us? Wife's name? Where exactly is Mr. Carter from?"

"Pittsburgh, Pennsylvania, Miss Crawford," O'Brien replied. "But he does have business interests here in Boston."

"I understand that our new Burroughs adding machines have been delivered," Jennifer said as she set about sending messages to the small kitchen for cakes, coffee, and hot water for brewing her tea.

"Yes, miss, they have," O'Brien said with a sparkle in her eye. "I am hoping we will be able to test them out today."

"I imagine we will. My father is sending another packet for us to examine."

"Yes, miss."

"Have you solved any of the mysteries of the Dorchester portfolio?"

"No, I have not, but I've got some ideas. Perhaps there'll be time later today for us to discuss them," O'Brien said.

Jennifer nodded and went to the sideboard, now being filled with trays of cakes and biscuits by a uniformed man, while O'Brien read aloud from a summary of Mr. Carter's holdings in the Crawford Bank and other notes that someone had written about his business ventures. Mr. Carter himself arrived shortly after, and O'Brien answered the knock on the door. Jennifer poured tea and commiserated with Mr. Carter over his fragile health. Wickers came a few scant minutes later and escorted Mr. Carter to her father's office.

"Well," Jennifer said as she rose. "That was quite simple today, wasn't it, O'Brien?"

"And quick, miss. Just as Mr. Carter was ready to explain every one of his ailments to you, Wickers came for him. A narrow escape," she said with a smile.

"I imagine you're right. Let's take a look at our new arithmetic machine, shall we?"

"Oh, yes," O'Brien said as she followed Jennifer into the office area. "But before we start with the new machine, I'd like to talk to you about the Dorchester portfolio while it's fresh in my brain."

"Yes. Let's begin with that. If my memory serves, Mr. Dorchester has a few outstanding loans against deposits held here at the bank and properties in the city," Jennifer said.

"That is correct. He has also bought a significant amount of stock certificates over the years, and as I looked at the purchases as recorded, I did some calculations and found that the percentage of the sales that the bank took was six percent, not five as we've seen on other occasions. Perhaps it means nothing," O'Brien said.

Jennifer took the green felt packet from O'Brien and untied the ribbon. She sat down at her desk and pulled out the contents. Individual packets of light yellow paper separated account tallies from stock certificates. Jennifer barely heard the click of the keys as O'Brien began testing the new adding machine as she was focused on the long column of numbers before her, and pulled out her tablet and pencil to make some calculations.

Thank heavens, the Ramsey School for Young Ladies curriculum included extensive mathematics classes. Jennifer had excelled in those classes and had been named the top student. Her father had allowed her access to his office when he was home in the evening and she remembered many nights standing by his side as a young girl, or sitting on his lap even, and tallying long lists of numbers, learning division and multiplication. He'd declared she had "a head for numbers" even better than his own and that it was such a pity she was a girl rather than a boy. But he'd said it with a smile and a hug and Jennifer didn't feel quite as bad as she might at what he'd said, because there was little doubt she was his favorite, even when Jillian still lived with them and was a perfect vision of beauty at a very young age.

A school friend from Ramsey was going to attend Mount Holyoke Female Seminary to pursue a degree in literature after her years at Ramsey were completed. Jennifer had asked her father and mother at the dinner table one evening if she would be allowed to attend with her classmate to further study mathematics. Her mother had scolded her beyond anything she could have imagined. Jennifer had been humiliated, and her father had reprimanded her for even bringing such a subject up to her mother and for making the whole family subject to Jane's tirades because of it. And indeed her mother continued to bring up the subject for years afterwards to relatives and friends, describing her daughter as having aspirations to be a spinster bluestocking to anyone who would listen.

Jennifer's cheeks colored with the remembrance of those grim days and what felt like constant embarrassment. But more than that, her relationship with her father, her stalwart champion and confidante, was damaged. They were no longer easy with each other in conversation and there was a coldness from him toward her after that. Jennifer was devastated. Then the influenza changed all their lives. Jolene's son, little William, dead from the disease and her first husband Turner gone as well, and Jolene no longer interested or able to go to the bank and entertain Crawford Bank clients in the parlor lobby.

Last year, an olive branch had been extended when her father agreed after some persuasion that she be allowed to accompany him to the bank a few days a week and continue what Jolene had begun. Then one day he'd arrived in the parlor lobby with a packet and a rather sheepish look on his face. She remembered the moment as if it were just occurring.

"I wonder if you'd take a look at this, Jennifer," he had said. "The bookkeepers have pored over this and none can find the errors, but it is a very complicated account." He looked up at her and smiled. "And then I recalled you were here in the building, and if anyone can unravel a mathematical mystery it is you. You've always been remarkably clever with numbers, even when you were a young girl. How proud I've always been of you."

Jennifer choked back a sob at the time and anytime since that she'd let herself repeat her father's words in her head. What a fine day that had been! She'd looked up at him and stretched out her hands to take the packet with a wide smile and glistening eyes. He'd hugged her in a loose embrace with a final pat on her back before releasing her. She'd reviewed the paperwork and saw within the first hour or so exactly what had happened and where the error had been made.

From that day onward, her father had brought her the most complicated of the account reviews that his staff of clerks and bookkeepers were unable to balance. She was fairly certain that no one else at the bank knew she and O'Brien were doing this sort of work. Jennifer did not care, not one little bit, that she was not to receive the credit for her discoveries, and more than that, she could never describe the elation she felt when facing hundreds of pages of entries, many so small that it was difficult to read them and some sloppily written, and the challenge of untangling those rows of digits.

Then occasionally, she would allow gloom to descend on her when faced with the reality that Jeffrey would be mortified if he ever knew she did this sort of thing, as it appeared that she actually worked for the bank, and he would never allow it if they married. This passion she felt for numbers would always transcend any passion he would elicit, even if intimate, she suspected. How lowering to feel less for the man she was intended to marry than for crinkled documents with an occasional tea stain.

Jennifer stopped her reminiscing as she scanned the final document and began a meticulous accounting of every stock certificate transaction listed. "Just as you said, not every stock sale garnered the bank six percent. Some were five percent. How odd. Wouldn't it make sense for the bank to charge the same percentage each time?"

"I don't really know," O'Brien said. "Is there someone we can ask?"

"My father, I suppose," Jennifer said. She pulled the stock certificates that the bank held in collateral from the folder and compared the hand-stamped serial numbers to the ones on the lists. "These ten were charged six percent and the remaining twenty-four were charged five percent. How odd. The dates are random, as well."

"Who signed off on the column entry?"

"Two of the six by two different clerks and four of them by the same clerk," Jennifer replied. "But the initials themselves are difficult to decipher."

"So three different clerks. If we can match the initials to a name, could we ask them why they charged six percent? Could your father?"

"I hesitate to ask my father before we can say something definitive. Perhaps there is a way to determine whose initials are whose," Jennifer said. "Let us think of way, O'Brien, without revealing why."

Chapter Two

"IT DOESN'T SEEM POSSIBLE THAT you've already been here a week, Zebidiah," Bella Moran said to her brother, seated at the dining room table in their family home in Athens, Georgia. "I will miss you more now that I have seen you again after these five years since mother's death."

"I'm going to get home more often, I promise," he replied.

Bella turned from the buffet where she poured her tea, and arched a brow. She carried her cup to the table and sat down across from her brother. "No, you will not. You have a life of your own, a very good one, and successful one, too, that will keep you very busy. And in our country's capital, no less, working for a United States senator."

"Don't make it out to be more than it is. I wonder if this whole thing is a fool's errand," he said.

"Fool's errand? I don't think even Father would say that to his cronies."

Zeb smiled ruefully. "I don't imagine Foster Cummings had anything good to say."

"He asked if you would be raising the Confederate flag when you got there."

"Sounds like him," Zeb said with a laugh. He looked at his sister then, all the levity and casualness gone from his face. "I should have moved back here after Mother died. I shouldn't have left you alone here to shoulder the burden. You should marry and have your own family, Bella. Not be saddled with taking care of Father."

She stared at him, and her face turned pink. "What a horrible thing to say, Zebidiah," she said with a shaking voice. "How dare you reduce my life to something pitiful and not of my own making? How dare you?"

"So you prefer this life, do you? You can't lie to me, Bella."

"Do you think I begrudge one minute, one second, of the time I spend helping Father with his work? I don't. I'm active and useful and respected. Not all women are so fortunate."

"From what I've seen this week, you have little to do with Father's research but have completely taken over Mother's tasks. You manage Melly and Victor and pay the household bills. I saw you yesterday talking to Jim Shaub about the leak in the roof. You told me yourself that you've taken over Mother's commitments at church, teaching Sunday School and serving on the Ladies Guild. When do you have time to do anything but manage this house?" he asked.

Bella stood and moved hastily to the window that overlooked the side yard where buds were just beginning to show on the trees. "I don't appreciate this, Zebidiah. Not one bit. What would you have me do?"

"I would have you have a life of your own. And our father should not be expecting you to fill Mother's shoes," he said quietly. "I blame him for this."

"Of course you do," Bella said without turning. "You have blamed our father for every mishap and misunderstanding in this house since you were a boy."

"Perhaps the blame should lie with him, Bella," he said. "But you have always defended him regardless of his culpability."

"Exactly what do you suggest, Zebidiah?"

Zeb thought about the realities of his family. At this point in Gordon Moran's life what were the chances that he could change? Very slim, Zeb imagined. His father's absentmindedness had been beloved by his mother. When Father couldn't find his shoes or didn't know the cost of beef or understand the work necessary to maintain a three-story home, Evelyn Moran had shrugged, smiled, and tenderly kissed her husband's forehead. Father never knew why Mother was fussing over him, or handing him matching socks, or even why workmen had to be pounding their hammers during the day in the room right next to his study, interrupting his work and concentration. Zeb had wanted to shout, and he did when he was older, screaming out his frustrations.

"I doubt it is realistic to imagine that Father would suddenly understand the realities of life. That there were things and people, his family specifically, that have needed his attention for years," Zeb said.

Bella seated herself across from him and looked at him with concern. "You still carry this anger with you, Zebidiah?"

He shook his head. "No, but I am worried about you. Will you look back and be regretful that you've not done something else with your life?"

"And you are certain this life," she said and swept her hand around the room, "is not of my own making? Perhaps not what I dreamed of when I was a young girl, but we all, each one of us, make compromises. I have considerable freedom here. I come and go as I please, associate with whomever I wish, and have the house budget at my disposal. There are advantages to having a father who does not pay much attention to everyday life."

He chuckled. "You make it sound as though you've got assignations with mysterious men at each turn."

"Hardly." Her face reddened and she stood quickly, turning to the buffet. She seated herself once again and put a plate of lace cookies between them. "And anyway, I'm an unmarried woman in 1893. Where exactly would I go, and how would I support myself if I left here? It is not done."

Bella was unnerved. That was something he'd rarely seen from his older sister. It was as if she *were* having assignations with mysterious men. Zeb could not contemplate that and did not wish to, in any event. She was an adult, as he'd just chided her, and he supposed she was entitled to her own secrets.

"Why don't you plan a trip to Washington?" he asked. "Mrs. Shelby has already sent word that she has found a house for me to rent."

Bella raised her brows. "Mrs. Shelby has put herself out and searched for lodgings for you? That is very kind. I gathered from your letters that she was rather coldhearted and that you were not fond of her."

"She is cold," Zeb said. "I pitied Max even with all her outward perfections. But she carried a lot of burdens from Boston, and there is no doubt I would be dead in my grave if it hadn't been for her."

"The influenza? Your letters led me to believe that you had rather a mild dose."

"That wasn't quite true," he said. "I didn't want to worry you, but I was close to death's door. She and her maid nursed me through the worst of it I understand, although I have no recollection of four full days."

"Four full days? Dear Lord!"

"Mrs. Shelby's sister was there, too," he said and shook his head. "Nearly as contrary and as ridiculous a woman as I've ever met."

"That's rather strong language about a woman who nursed you. Is she much like her sister the senator's wife?"

Zeb shrugged. He'd asked Miss Crawford to take a turn with him in the garden after having dinner at the Hacienda with Senator and Mrs. Shelby before he'd left for Georgia. He'd asked her straight out where she'd gotten the bruises he'd seen on her side the night his fever broke.

Zeb looked away and saw in his mind's eye what he'd seen that night from the cot in the new bunkhouse where Mrs. Shelby had nursed the sick. It was as if he'd been swimming through thick water until he finally broke the surface and opened his eyes. His throat was dry and his mouth tasted foul, but he realized he was alive and that the empty cots beside him meant others had recovered or were dead. Jennifer Crawford was standing near a glass window in a darkened corner directly in his line of sight, her face in shadows, moonlight drifting over one of her shoulders and down her side. He'd watched her remove her blouse and untie the strings of her corset. She held herself stiffly as the corset fell away and took a long, and clearly painful, deep breath. She lifted her chemise and turned, letting the moonlight illuminate her bare side. He'd concentrated at first on the outline of her breast and the shadow it cast. But then he looked at her side and the ridges of her ribs. She was covered in bruises, some black, and some fading. She touched the center of a particularly large one and hissed in pain. When she realized he watched her, she said he was "ungentlemanly," something her sister had said about him on occasion.

"She denied it all," he said. "As if I had dreamed it all. I did not dream it."

"Dream what?" Bella asked.

Zeb looked up and realized he'd spoken aloud. He shook his head. "Nothing. It was nothing."

But he was long gone then in his recall of Jennifer Crawford. He did not notice his sister leave the room but was picturing Jennifer as she looked at him in the garden that night. She was as gorgeous a woman as he'd ever laid eyes on, contrary to his long-held notion that Southern belles were the most beautiful, charming females in the country. It wasn't just her looks, he thought, although her green eyes and dark blond hair with just a hint of auburn were a perfect feminine combination, but rather an ethereal fragility that drew him. Outwardly she was kind and had the confident ease gained when one is well-educated and wealthy. But if the eyes truly were the window to one's soul, then he would describe her as damaged.

Jennifer was wary, and guarded herself, her real self, as if she were being hunted. And perhaps that is exactly what the ugly bruises on her side represented. She'd been face to face with a nemesis and not been the victor. Zeb thought about the man who laid fists on her fair skin, undoubtedly placed where few if any would see them, and considered how he would kill him.

* * *

"What do you think of this one, Mr. Moran?" the tailor asked.

Bella had taken one look at the shirts he wore and the pants he gave Melly to wash and told him he was to go to Taitlinger's immediately in order to give them enough time to make him appropriate clothing for his new employment. She would not have her brother humiliate and degrade the Moran name by showing up at the Capital in a flannel shirt and dungarees. He agreed reluctantly, and she accompanied him on his first trip and did the ordering herself.

"It looks fine to me," he said, turning from side to side in front of the huge mirror at the back of the shop. "How many did Miss Moran order?"

"Eleven complete suits, shirts, undergarments . . ."

"Eleven? What? I don't need eleven suits!"

"That does not count the formal wear, sir. And she insisted on the new design from New York." The tailor paused. "The tuxedo jacket. It is the first one I have made!"

"How am I going to get all this stuff to Washington?" Zeb asked.

"Miss Moran told me that you are to be working for a U.S. senator, sir, and instructed me to purchase a trunk and pack all but the light-colored suit since it would be appropriate for travel."

"Did she really?"

"Yes, and the shoemaker has some ready-to-wear shoes that he will be bringing by shortly for you to try on."

Zeb shook his head. "No. That's it. I'm not giving up my boots. I don't care what anyone thinks."

The tailor nodded. "Miss Moran said you'd say that and instructed me to have the cobbler bring dark boots for you to try on since the only pair she's seen of yours are light-colored and those would look ridiculous with evening wear. Her words, not mine."

"I'm not surprised," Zeb said. "I suppose I should get a haircut and a trim, too?"

"Miss Moran told me to mention that there was a barber just a few doors down."

"What did Miss Moran have to say about what all this stuff's going to cost?" Zeb asked.

"She said you had plenty enough money to begin dressing like a gentleman."

"She would say that." Zeb sucked in a breath at the amount on the tally sheet the tailor handed him. It seemed like a huge waste, but then what did he know? He certainly did not want to embarrass Max, and it was better that his sister admonished him than Mrs. Shelby, who would do the same thing that Bella had if she did not think what he was wearing was appropriate.

* * *

"You'll want to get that breath of air now, Jennifer," Jeffrey Rothchild said as he stood up from his chair in the Crawford Bank's box at the Boston Theatre. He held his hand out to help her stand.

Jennifer looked at his hand and then his face. She had not mentioned wanting to leave her seat and was actually quite comfortable as they waited for the second act to begin. She was wary but then chided herself for being suspect of an apparently innocent request. Maybe she had mentioned earlier that she would like to mingle with other guests at some point. Maybe he was trying to make her happy. She placed her gloved hand in his and stood up.

"Thank you, Jeffrey," she said. "It is somewhat stuffy."

They walked down the wide circular hallway, greeting those they knew. Suddenly, Jeffrey grabbed her upper arm, lifting her nearly off of her feet, and pushed her through a doorway into a small closet. There was little light except the glow of a gas lamp through the window, and she smelled the odor of cleaning solutions.

"Jeffrey!" she said. "You are hurting my arm. Please!"

He twisted her roughly to face him and held her tightly with his left hand. "Your mother let me know that you are still planning this trip to Washington. I thought we'd settled that."

"Well," she said, and swallowed, "Father did say he would make my excuses . . . *aaahh*." Jeffrey slammed a closed fist into her ribs, just below her breast on the same side he pummeled before her trip to Texas. She reeled but he held her upright in his embrace.

He stroked her face and she flinched. "There is no need to put yourself through all this pain, my dear."

"I did not . . . I mean I . . ." she said between gasps.

"You meant to tell me that you won't be going to Washington, isn't that right, dear?"

Jennifer closed her eyes and nodded, breathing through her nose, and concentrated on not vomiting.

"Good," he said, and smiled. He opened the door to the closet and looked at her. "Your hair is mussed, Jennifer. It looks like I've just stolen a kiss."

She preceded him through the door on shaky legs, holding her arm tightly against her side and willing the pain to subside. He took her free arm through his and held her hand. He smiled at her affectionately as they moved down the hall toward her parents' box. The first person she saw was Evelyn Prentiss, an old friend of her mother's. Mrs. Prentiss sidled over to Jennifer, and whispered in ear.

"Smile, dear. And smooth your chignon. We don't want your mother and father to get an idea as to why you were in a cupboard with Mr. Rothchild," Mrs. Prentiss said with a conspiratorial grin.

Jennifer wobbled a smile and batted her lashes. Not to be coy, but to forestall the tears that were near to running down her face. She reached up to touch her hair and drew a sharp breath from the pain as she did so.

"Do not fret, Jennifer. I will say nothing to Jane," Mrs. Prentiss said. "Mum's the word!"

Jennifer watched Mrs. Prentiss rejoin her party. "I believe I am going to faint," she said.

Jeffrey began leading her down the hallway and leaned close to her. His nearness sent a shiver down her spine.

"Don't be a ninny, Jennifer. The Crawford box is right there."

Jeffrey opened the door to the bank's theatre box and seated her. Her father leaned forward. "Are you unwell, Jennifer? You are ghastly white."

She looked up at Jeffrey from under her lashes. He was staring at her intensely and nodded as if to prompt her reply. Oh, how she wished she could tell her father! She'd like to scream it on the street that Jeffrey Rothchild was brutal and a bully. But she did not. She could not be so brash and embarrass her father and the bank in such a public way. But she would not marry him, not even with the public announcements of his intentions, or her mother's cajoling and interfering. She would find a way to end this privately, with no public repercussions and unpleasantness.

"I am fine, Father," she said. "Perhaps just chilled."

"Would you like my topcoat, dear?" her father asked. "I will have the usher get it from the checkroom if you would like."

"No, Father, I'll be fine," she said as Jeffrey sat down beside her and leaned close to whisper in her ear.

"Did I tell you you look exceptionally beautiful tonight? I hope you are feeling better after your . . . accident. It worries me greatly that you may be unwell. I am going to send you vases of fresh flowers to brighten your day tomorrow. Would you like that?"

She nodded and turned to her parents seated behind her with as much of a bright smile as she could muster. "The play is beginning again!"

* * *

Jennifer asked a maid she met in the hallway as she went to her bedroom that evening to bring her ice. She had dismissed Eliza immediately upon coming into her room and would not meet her maid's eyes. When it happened before, the first time, she'd cried in her maid's arms on her return from Texas, wondering what she'd ever done to deserve such treatment. But when she'd dried her tears that night, she didn't feel relieved that she'd shared the story with Eliza, but rather humiliated. And while she was at odds as to how to end this relationship, and her mother was not only cruel and unpleasant, but ill as well, and her father was continuously manipulated, and her sisters had left her here, left her to manage the family, with all of that, she still had her pride.

* * *

"There are still teaching positions open here, Zebidiah, and one full professorship, I've been told at the Atlanta School. Why don't you get serious with your life?" Gordon Moran said.

"Father!" Bella admonished.

"What is it, Bella?" her father asked.

Zeb shook his head at his sister and looked at his father. He would soon be getting on the train, and Bella did not need to argue on his behalf and put herself at odds with her father. "I'm not going to teach, Father, anywhere. I've told you that as recently as last night. I was never interested in it, as you know."

"Certainly there is some other means of employment other than working for this . . . fellow," Father said.

"Senator Maximillian Shelby is his name. You would have me sweeping floors before you'd be happy I was working for a U.S. senator?"

"There's a godliness about labor, son, if you are not called to academics."

"And working for a U.S. senator, being involved in the direction our country takes, is a step down?"

Professor Moran turned as the whistle on the approaching train blew. "It's this man. This Shelby person." He looked at Zeb with consternation. "He's from Boston, Zebidiah. He's a Yankee. What could you possibly be thinking?"

Zeb saw the train slowing, saw passengers picking up their bags, and knew that he would be boarding soon.

Leave it, Zebidiah. But he could not after all leave it, as he'd done since forever.

"A Yankee? It's near thirty years since the War between the States was fought. It is long over."

Gordon Moran's face turned red, and he exerted himself enough to shake a finger in his son's face. "Over? It will never be over for a true Southerner!"

"You'd have colored folk like Melly and Victor slaves again?"

"We lost life with that war, not just honorable men, mind you, but our *way* of life. The South was stripped of its very essence."

"Perhaps, Father, if a majority of Southerners had recognized the brutality and evilness of slavery, instead of filling their pockets with the money made from those slaves' free labor and justifying the rape of the women, they could have begun to dismantle a system that was abhorrent on their own. But they did not. Southerners like you were not only cruel, but shortsighted as well. And to think an educated man like yourself still considers the ashed remnants of this abomination called the Confederacy, losing good men for the sake of whipping others, to be the standard, the bulwark. You're a sad, twisted old man without the veneer of mother's kindness."

Gordon Moran's face had paled. Bella's hand covered her mouth. Zeb had said aloud all the things that he'd said privately to himself over the years after clashes with his father. All the reasons he hated Georgia and many

Southerners' reticence to move on to a new day. But this was not the time or the place to deliver this message. Was there ever an appropriate time to reduce a parent's existence to this? He'd been shouting as well, and although the slowly chugging train masked most of his tirade, some people standing close by were staring at the three of him. He cleared his throat.

"Father. I am sorry to have shouted and said what I did. It was uncalled for." He turned to his sister. "My apologies, Bella."

"I'd hoped to have your leave-taking be more pleasant than last time, Zebidiah," she said. "Not that I don't completely agree with everything you said."

His father looked at her and back at him. It struck Zeb then that his father looked old, and forlorn as well, as if his foundations had shifted. The conductors had stepped off the stopped train and were helping passengers board. Zeb knew he must soon leave and that he must right this somehow.

"Your mother would be ashamed of you," his father said.

Bella slipped her arm through her father's and smiled. "She would have, not that she'd disagreed with anything Zebidiah has said, but rather that there is never a call to publically air our family squabbles, isn't that right?"

Zeb smiled. "You are right. It was indecorous of me. My sincere apologies. I love you both," he said, and kissed his sister's cheek. He held out his hand to his father.

"Go ahead, Father," Bella said and winked at Zeb. "Show your son how a true Southern gentleman behaves."

Gordon Moran straightened and stuck out his hand. Zeb shook it and held on to it for a long minute. "I will see you all soon, God willing. Take care." He turned and boarded the train as his trunk and cases were being loaded.

Chapter Three

"I FEEL LIKE A THIEF, running in the dead of night," Jennifer said to her maid, Eliza.

"Yes, miss," Eliza said, as she continued to move furniture in Jennifer's dressing room to make room for her trunk.

"And this groomsman is reliable?"

"He is, miss. I can attest for Luther myself as his family grew up beside mine. I've known him all my life. He reads and writes and can take direction, and he's always been half in love with me," Eliza said unashamedly. "'Tis a pity he's still wet behind the ears as he's turned out to be a handsome, strapping thing."

Jennifer smiled. "Eliza! I don't wish to take advantage of your friendship with him."

"I have promised him a kiss if he does exactly what I tell him to do."

Jennifer sat down on the chaise in her dressing room. She looked at her maid. "He hit me again, Eliza."

"Yes, miss. I know. I wondered when you dismissed me without me helping you change after the theatre last week, and then I saw your face as you lifted your arms so I could drop your day dress over your head the next morning." Eliza straightened and looked over her shoulder at Jennifer. "Is the rib broken like the last time?"

Jennifer shook her head. "I don't believe so."

She closed the lid of the trunk and sat an open valise on top of it. "Almost done here, miss, and then we will decide what you will wear to travel. Have you sent a message to your sister?"

Jennifer stared at her hands and listened to Eliza talk on about whether her leather shoes would go well enough with two of her evening dresses or whether she should pack the satin slippers that had been died to match her gowns. "I didn't tell you because I'm embarrassed," she said finally.

Eliza straightened. "I've always been too forward for a maid in service, but there's no changing me now. But I will gladly peel potatoes for the rest of my employment in this house rather than not say my piece about this."

"Say whatever it is you want to say. I realize I'm a fool."

Eliza hurried to her and knelt in front of her. She clutched her hands. "No, Miss Jennifer. You must never speak like that. Don't you see? That is what he wants. He is counting on you blaming yourself. And each time it happens, you'll blame yourself a little more, until you're certain that it is your fault and you deserve his fists. Don't give into it, miss!"

Jennifer wiped her eyes. "I have no idea how I ended up in this situation. When it happened the first time, I was caught so unaware. I didn't know what to say or who to say it to. And I had convinced myself that it was just that one time and that he was tired and I'd been vexing him."

"It's never right to hit another person, my granny would say, and I think it's true even when you're tired."

"Yes. You are right, Eliza," she said.

"Have you told Mr. Crawford?"

Jennifer shook her head. "I'm not sure what he would do. Mr. Rothchild is an employee of the bank. There'd be talk. And it would make it so awkward between him and Mother. I hate to put him in that position."

"But you must tell someone, miss. You must. I don't think Mr. Rothchild will just walk away if you tell him that you do not want to marry him."

"There is a person I'm going to tell, Eliza. Don't worry. My sister Jolene will know what to do."

* * *

"Have you told your mother that you're leaving today?" Jennifer's father asked her the following day from where he sat across from her in the dining room at Willow Tree.

"She was not up when I stopped by her rooms. I told Eliza to tell Mildred I was going out."

Her father stared at her. "Is Eliza going to tell Mildred you'll be boarding the train for Washington?"

"Not exactly."

"And do you think your mother will not notice if you are gone for more than one day, perhaps even a month, as you originally planned?"

"I'm sorry, Father. I'm a coward. I don't want to listen to Mother drone on about Jeffrey and about the Morgans' party," Jennifer said, and looked up at him with pleading eyes. "I was hoping you'd tell her."

"What did Jeffrey say? He was a bit high-handed that night at dinner, I thought."

Jennifer stood and poured herself a cup of tea. "I have not told him, either."

"You have not told your intended?"

"He is not my intended," she said quickly. "I have never said that I would marry him. He and Mother will not decide this for me. I have left him a note, though, that will be delivered tomorrow morning."

"There is a bank meeting here this morning in my library. Jeffrey will be one of the members. Will he not see your trunks and cases and wonder?"

"My trunks and cases went on yesterday's train with one of the groomsmen. I checked with Bellings first, of course."

He shook his head and chuckled. "Quite an elaborate scheme, my dear! Just tell Jeffrey that you have had a change of heart. He is a gentleman. He will be gracious about it, and I believe your mother exaggerates when she says that you and Jeffrey are discussed as a betrothed couple in drawing rooms."

Jennifer nearly blurted out her fears but did not. *What a coward I am!* she thought. *I cannot even tell my father, who loves me dearly, that I am afraid that Jeffrey would be everything but a gentleman.* She rose and kissed his cheek. "I have written a kind but firm letter to him. And if I'm gone for some days then it will be easier when we see each other again at the bank or at a social affair. Some time will have passed and perhaps meeting him won't be so awkward."

"You believe Jeffrey's feelings are more engaged than yours?"

Jennifer hesitated. "I believe Jeffrey is accustomed to having his own way."

Her father folded his newspaper and touched her hand, although he did not look at her. "Please tell Jolene that I am happy for her and the senator. I do not believe business will allow me to come to Washington for his swearing in but I am thinking of her and him with pride."

Her eyes filled with tears. "You should try and come, father. Jolene has not heard from Julia, but if she and her husband are coming you would have a chance to see

Jillian and meet your other grandchildren, Jacob and Mary Lou. I am praying that Julia decides to make the trip. I am anxious to meet her husband and see the children."

"We will see how your mother is feeling then," he said with resignation. "Although I would like to speak to Julia and her husband again. I foolishly allowed your mother to convince me to do some things that I'm not proud of. I would like to apologize in person although I have done it by letter."

The door to the dining room opened and Bellings stepped inside. "The carriage is here for you whenever you are ready, Miss Crawford. Mr. Crawford? Gentlemen have begun to arrive for your meeting. I have shown them to the library. Coffee is being served."

Jennifer walked arm in arm with her father to the foyer. Eliza was already in the carriage, and Bellings helped her on with her coat. Jeffrey arrived just then.

"My dear. You are a vision of beauty and refinement. How fortunate I am," he said as he came forward with a smile, gathering her hands in his. He noticed her coat. "Where are you off to? I saw your maid in the carriage. Is there something I could assist you with?"

Jennifer withdrew her hands and pulled on her gloves. "Not unless you'd like to shop for hats, and then I will be stopping at the Lending Library. I'm also meeting some friends for luncheon at the Parker House Hotel."

Jeffrey stared at her and spoke quietly as her father greeted other guests. "What friends will you be meeting? Do I know any of them?"

"I don't think you do know them. I went to Ramsey with them, and we get together from time to time."

"What are their names? Perhaps I do know them."

"We're getting ready to begin the meeting, Jeffrey," her father said as he kissed Jennifer's cheek. "Run along Jennifer. It will be quite late as is until you are back from all of your errands." He put his hand on Jeffrey's back as he guided him down the hallway. Jeffrey turned to stare at her one last time, and the look he gave her sent shivers down her spine.

* * *

Zeb stepped off the train onto the B&O station platform, thankful to be off the locomotive after three days of near nonstop travel. He moved through the throngs of people to where a porter was unloading trunks and bags. The stationmaster pointed to where men with wagons and buggies were loading luggage and people. He found a free one and handed the man the address of the house that Jolene had let for him. He wondered if there would be a grocer nearby or a restaurant at least. He was tired of eating his meals out of wrapped paper as he'd done on the trip and was looking forward to sitting down at a table with a fork and knife and a real plate. And then he wondered if this house was even furnished. He might be sleeping on the floor!

The driver *whoahed* the buggy in a neighborhood of connected brick houses, all three stories high, some shutters painted red, some white, and some black. He matched the brass numbers beside the white door under a shingled roof to the ones on Jolene's letter. Zeb looked up and down the street and thought it looked like a fairly prosperous neighborhood and noticed a well-dressed woman pushing a baby in a cart on the wide, tree-lined sidewalk. The driver began to unload his trunks when the front door of his Seventeenth Street home opened. A formally dressed man came out the door.

"Mr. Moran?" Zeb nodded, and the man continued. "I am Smithers. Senator Shelby's wife has hired me as a valet and general houseman for you." Smithers looked at the man pulling Zeb's trunks off of the back of the buggy he rode in and went down the steps to help carry them and the bags. "Help me carry these to the second floor, now, my man."

Zeb followed the men inside and watched as Smithers pulled change from his pocket to tip the driver and closed the door. Smithers turned to him.

"Of course, this arrangement is temporary for us. Once you have settled you may have your own staff that you would wish to join you," Smithers said. "Allow me to take your coat, sir. Would you like to see the house first, or perhaps you would like to go to your rooms?"

Zeb looked around. "Is there an office or a library here with a desk?"

"Yes, sir," Smithers said, and led him down the hallway. "Here you are, sir."

Zeb stepped inside and looked around. The room was everything he'd dreamed of having for himself. There was a large library in his father's house that was always his father's domain. He'd never felt comfortable there even when studying during his years at university. He'd had a large bedroom and sitting room of his own at the Hacienda when he'd lived there and worked for Max, and he had cleaned those rooms himself rather than allowing one of the staff to do it. This room wasn't huge but had a large fireplace, floor-to-ceiling books on shelves, and a large desk beside a stately, paned window. He walked to the desk, touched the felt pad, and sat down on the chair behind it.

"Smithers?" he said. "Tell me more about this arrangement."

"I was hired by Mrs. Shelby, as I said earlier, to be valet and manage the house for you. Mrs. Shelby has advised that I hire a cook and a maid and perhaps an all-about boy. I have hired all three and they are ready to meet you if you wish."

Zeb shook his head. "I don't want to put anyone out of a job, but I just don't see myself needing anyone other than someone to clean once in a while and maybe take the laundry."

"Certainly, sir. I'll inform the staff. I was quite clear when I hired them that this might not be permanent."

"What is this?" Zeb asked as he picked up an envelope addressed to Chief of Staff with a lone sheet of paper inside.

"I believe that is your calendar for the next few weeks, sir. A gentleman from Senator Shelby's office brought it," Smithers said. "If it is acceptable to you, I want to inform the rest of the staff that they will be leaving tomorrow. Excuse me, sir."

Zeb scanned the document and held a hand up. "Wait. Smithers. Wait." In the first week alone, he would be attending functions on three evenings and was expected to entertain small parties on two other evenings. The guest list for the second party included the assistant secretary of state. His first scheduled appointment was for six thirty the next morning, followed by a full complement of tours, meetings, and appointments. "From the looks of this, you'll be staying, Smithers, and so will anyone else you've hired. Have you read this?"

"Certainly not, sir."

Zeb stared at the man. "But why do I get the feeling you knew you weren't going anywhere?"

"Mrs. Shelby did say that you would not be open to this idea until you saw your calendar."

"Did she now? It appears that I'll barely have time to sleep and shave let alone cook or keep up with household work. I'm unaccustomed to this sort of thing, Smithers. I grew up in a prosperous home in Georgia with cooks and some weekly cleaning help, but nothing like this. You will have to give me some time to become adjusted."

"Certainly, sir. Please make your wishes known so that we may be able to serve you in the best fashion, as we will want to make sure that your household is suitable for such an important man as yourself."

"Important?" Zeb said and *harrumphed*. "Hardly. I'm just here to help Senator Shelby."

"Of course, sir. Allow me to show you the rest of the house."

The furnishings, as much as he could judge, were discreetly expensive, and impressive, mostly done in some combination of dark blue and tan. "Did this house come with all the furniture and the pictures and carpets?"

Smithers shook his head. "No, sir, not completely. Some rooms were bare on the lower floor, but the sleeping rooms and the staff quarters furnishings were all included in the sale of the house according to Mrs. Shelby."

"And where did the furnishings on the lower floor come from, Smithers?"

"The senator's wife chose the furnishings. She told me to tell you the bills would be arriving here for payment, sir."

"Damnation!" Zeb said. "How much of my money has she spent? I suppose she anticipated this reaction as well."

"She did, sir, and I would be more comfortable if Mrs. Shelby relayed the amount to you in person."

Zeb was seated at the dining room table at one of the sixteen chairs and served his dinner while Smithers unpacked his trunk and other bags in his rooms, even after he insisted that he preferred to eat in his library at his desk or in the kitchen in the small alcove where the staff ate their meals. Zeb fell asleep in his new bed as he read and reread the U.S. Constitution and the accompanying Articles.

Chapter Four

"AUNT JENNIFER!" MELINDA SHOUTED, AND ran full tilt at her across the black and white tiled floor of Jolene's Washington home. "I have been waiting forever!"

Jennifer hugged Melinda and kissed her hair. "It does seem like forever, doesn't it?"

"Let your aunt breathe, Melinda," Jolene said as she made her way across the foyer. "How was your trip?"

"Uneventful," Jennifer said, and looked Jolene up and down. "What is different?"

Jolene linked her arm through Jennifer's. "Let me show you to your rooms and allow Mrs. Trundle to help your maid get you both settled. Finish your studies,

Melinda, and then you may have unfettered access to your aunt."

Jennifer followed the young men carrying her trunks and bags into a spacious, high-ceilinged room with long windows and a massive bed.

"How lovely, Jolene! You must have been very busy, as your last letter said you were considering moving to a hotel until the work was done here."

"It has been an incredible rush but well worth it, I think," Jolene said as she straightened drapes and ran her hand along a tall dresser. She turned to her housekeeper. "Please have a tea tray sent up and perhaps some cakes, as well."

"That sounds lovely," Jennifer said as she unpinned her hat.

"You are probably tired," Jolene said. "Take a rest and we'll talk when you are ready."

"No, no," Jennifer said, and pointed to two flowered chairs in front of a marble fireplace. "Sit down with me here. Tell me what is happening. I'm very excited for you and Max, and you are looking more beautiful than usual, Jolene. Your dress is lovely."

"We'll go to the dressmakers while you are here, if you'd like. I've found a dress shop that is extraordinary, and I'll be there quite a bit as I will be needing all new things."

"All new, Jolene? I was at the Hacienda when Alice packed you. If I remember correctly there were eleven trunks."

"But I won't fit in those dresses very shortly, Jennifer," she said and smiled. "Maximillian and I are expecting a son or daughter this fall."

"I am so happy for you both!" Jennifer cried, and stood to kiss her sisters' cheek. "What wonderful news!"

"It is wonderful news. I never thought I'd feel so much joy. I never thought I could feel true happiness ever again. But I can and I do."

Jennifer blinked back tears. "Of course you can. What did Max say?"

"He is nearly beside himself and is so busy with the Senate, but he sends me messages by courier at all hours and has told the staff that I am to do nothing strenuous, as if I were scrubbing floors, and Melinda tattles on me to her father. The minx!"

Jennifer was in awe of her sister's transformation. This unguarded Jolene was nothing as she remembered, not as her sister was while growing up at Willow Tree, and definitely not during her first marriage. When her son, William, died, Jolene descended further into her own misery, Jennifer had always thought, never smiling, speaking rarely, and when she did it was often a biting, and, on occasion, even cruel remark. Jennifer had not been looking forward to visiting Jolene and her new husband in Texas, but she desperately needed time away from her mother and put aside her fears and worries about traveling that distance to a sister who was not particularly a happy person and went anyway. She arrived in the midst of the influenza outbreak at the ranch, but even then, during their worry for Melinda and all the others at the ranch, she could see that Jolene had changed.

"You look like and act like a different person. I am very, very happy for you."

Jolene stared at her sister. "But you do not look happy. In fact, you look quite miserable, Jennifer. What is it? Is it Mother? I have told you and will continue to tell you that you are welcome to make your life here with us. Maximillian has told me to impress upon you that he would be happy to have you live with us indefinitely."

"But it isn't always that easy. I don't know what Father has said to you, but Mother is ill. She will not tell me or Father the details but the doctor has examined her."

"And you believe it is serious?"

"I do. And I will not abandon Father to her tantrums."

Jennifer sat silently staring into the fire and calming her racing heart. She was near tears and not quite sure why.

"I have never thought about how this has affected you, Jennifer. I'm sure Julia did not either. But you must feel as though we've left you there," Jolene said softly, breaking the silence.

"Everyone is free to live their own life. You have moved on and are happy, and I am glad for you."

"Except you, Jennifer. Are you free to live your own life?"

Jennifer swallowed, feeling angry and tense but hardly willing to upset this new balance between her and Jolene. She jumped up from her chair and hurried to the window. "What a lovely view, Jolene. This house compares to Landonmore in many ways. You must be very pleased."

Jolene came to stand beside her and pushed the curtain back to look out herself. "I am very pleased and very fortunate. Now, I'm sure you're exhausted. I'll send your maid to you."

* * *

"She's finally here, Melinda!" Max said, and wrapped Jennifer in a bear hug and then kissed both of her cheeks. "I am so glad you're here. Jolene and Melinda have done nothing but complain that you were not with us when we arrived."

Jennifer smiled and held Max's hands in hers. "I've heard that you are to be a papa again and I am thrilled for you!"

Max nodded, and Jennifer was certain she saw his eyes glisten with tears.

"I am terrified something will go wrong and worry about her and the baby constantly, but the doctor says that she is healthy and fit and he foresees no problems."

"You must think good thoughts, Max. Jolene had no issues when she delivered William, and my sister Julia has birthed three healthy children."

"You are right," he said and wrapped her arm around his to lead her to the dining room. "But I can't help worrying about her and Melinda and this new child."

"Of course you can't," Jennifer said as she was seated. "You are as smitten with my sister as I remember, and your daughter has you wrapped around her finger."

Max laughed.

"I heard from your sister today, Maximillian. She and Calvin will be here for the ceremonies," Jolene said.

"Excellent. I haven't seen Eugenia in ages and I want to personally thank her for introducing Jolene and I," Max said. "Do you remember when your Aunt Eugenia and Uncle Calvin visited with us at the Hacienda, Melinda?"

"A little," Melinda said. "Especially that hat that Aunt Eugenia wore with the pink flowers and the printed ribbons."

"Your Aunt Eugenia is a bit eccentric in her clothing choices, but your father is right. She introduced us and we will always be eternally grateful," Jolene said as she looked steadily at her husband. "I shall have to tell the foreman that I need the green bedroom suite ready in time for them."

"Are my parents coming?" Max asked.

"No. Eugenia said they are disappointed but your father is not feeling well and your mother is concerned about him making the trip."

"With this schedule they've got me on already, I doubt I'll have time to travel anywhere until the session closes, and Mother and Father are getting up in years," Max said as he filled his plate from the platters the servants were presenting.

"Then I shall go meet and visit with your parents this spring and take Melinda with me. It is long past—" Jolene began.

Max shook his head. "No. Absolutely not. You will not be traveling."

Jolene laid down her silverware and arched her brows. "Perhaps we should discuss this at another time when you are not so . . . passionate about the subject."

Melinda giggled, and Jolene looked at her until she was silent and took a fork full of food to her mouth.

"Father has written that you have reopened the parlor lobby at the bank," Jolene said to Jennifer.

"I have and have found your notes to be particularly useful when we are entertaining a long-term client."

"The parlor lobby?" Max asked.

Jolene nodded. "When I was married to Turner, I entertained clients before they met with my father or other bank employees in a comfortable room with a private entrance. It started out when I overheard Father telling his secretary that the week ahead was going to be very busy and he was concerned that he and his staff were not going to be able to take care of all the customers coming to see him in a timely manner."

"Mother was in a foul temper about it if I remember correctly," Jennifer said.

"Mother was often in a foul temper," Jolene replied. "Anyway, I went to work with my father that week, with a maid of course, and served coffee and tea and cakes from a pastry shop around the corner from the bank to clients who were going to be delayed because my father was running late with a previous appointment. I made polite conversation and kept notes so I would know what to ask or comment on the next time the client visited."

"Father said half the reason the bank was doing so well was because Jolene was greeting customers," Jennifer said.

"Men are notoriously silly when it comes to appearances. As if I had the foggiest notion of the business of banking. However, after playing hostess there for some years, I was much acquainted with how and why things worked the way they did behind the scenes."

"Of course you did," Max said, and waved his fork. "I have said all along that you are very business savvy and bright. Obviously your father recognized that."

"I would like to work somewhere when I grow up," Melinda said.

Max grumbled.

"You will, Melinda," Jolene said. "You will be managing the Shelby family's considerable holdings in property and investments, and preparing the next generation, and your sister or brother, to help you."

"That is not the same," Melinda whined.

"What would you like to do when it is time to decide?" Jolene asked.

Nothing in this conversation or in the energy surrounding it was anything like the family dinners at Willow Tree, now often just Mother, Father, and her, and done mostly in silence, other than when Mother berated someone in her sphere. The great knot in Jennifer's stomach was slowly unwinding. How calming it would be to not have constant tension, to relax and not be so wary. She awoke from her thoughts when Max spoke to her.

"Jolene says that according to your father, a certain gentleman has become a favorite of yours. When will we get to meet him?"

Her peace was interrupted even without his name being mentioned. How would she ever escape him? Would she ever have this comfort that she felt with Jolene's family as her own? She looked up at Max.

"He is *not* my favorite, and I have recently told Father so."

Jennifer concentrated on her meal then and keeping her hands from shaking as she reached for her wineglass. Max excused himself early to meet with a fellow senator, and Jolene gave her an extensive tour of the house, from the attics to the staff quarters. Melinda held her hand and swung their arms between them as if they did not have a care in the world. When they came to Melinda's rooms, she asked if she could stay behind from the rest of the tour as she was still arranging them to her liking.

"Of course," Jolene said to her and kissed her forehead. "Young ladies like to have their things just so."

"You and Melinda seem quite affectionate," Jennifer said as they settled themselves into comfortable chairs in Jolene's private rooms.

"We are. It is quite astonishing to you, I imagine, knowing how we were with Mother growing up."

Jennifer nodded. "It seems as though that is the way it is supposed to be. I remember going to my friend Ruth Edgewood's house and sometimes eating dinner with them when Mother allowed it. The Edgewoods talked about all kinds of interesting things and there was always laughter and . . . well, it always made me wonder why our family dinners were not like that."

"I am very fortunate to have found Maximillian. He has drawn me into viewing life from a much different perspective. He is happy that he is alive and that Melinda is well and that he married me . . . although sometimes I wonder." Jolene stopped and dabbed her eyes. "I am an emotional mess with this impending motherhood."

"I am glad for you."

Jolene nodded. "It all makes me think of little William, and makes me alternately joyful and terrified. But Maximillian is my bulwark. He tells people about our son William and that we lost him to the influenza. He acts as if he was William's father, and when I questioned him he told me that I birthed and loved William and therefore he loves him because he loves me. He said that I consider Melinda my daughter, and why shouldn't he consider William his son? What am I to say in the face of that resolve?"

"He is a very special person."

"He is," Jolene agreed and sipped a cold tea, and then turned in her chair to face Jennifer. "Your response to Maximillian at dinner when he mentioned Jeffrey Rothchild leads me to believe he is less than special."

Jennifer sat in silence, listening to the crack of the fire as logs broke and watching their sparks fly. "He is not special at all. In fact, he is not a pleasant man."

"In what ways, Jennifer? Has he been unkind or ungentlemanly?" Jolene asked with a keen eye.

She did not know why but she was unwilling to share this humiliation with Jolene, as she had planned. She was embarrassed, for certain, but that was not the whole of it. Ghastly as it seemed, there was a small voice whispering to her that perhaps she deserved whatever punishment Jeffrey saw fit to deliver. Perhaps she *was* in the wrong. Perhaps that was the reason that everyone in her family had deserted her in one way or another.

"He is not a good person, Jolene, but it is unnecessary for you to be concerned. Maybe I have given into hysterics."

"It is absolutely necessary for me to be concerned. I had problems and tragedies in my life and managed them alone, with little success I later learned. Julia had problems, too, and she managed them alone and could have ended up married to a man who beat her or killed her. Thankfully she married an honorable man who adores her and *all* of their children. I have come to realize, like you, that our family did not function as it should have as we grew up. Maximillian would never let someone struggle alone or in desperation. If his sister telegraphed him that she was having a problem he would walk off the Senate floor in that instant, even if President Cleveland himself were in conversation with him. I have found that an outward-looking psyche is healthy, and that constant and never-ending secretiveness and internalization are not."

"They may not be, but secretively is how we function at Willow Tree."

"It does make one susceptible to unpleasantness if surrounded by unpleasant people. That is why I have urged you repeatedly to live with us indefinitely."

"I cannot."

"But why not? I know that Turner left you a lump sum in his will. Between that and what Father would give you, you would certainly have a comfortable income."

"It is not the money, Jolene. I live a relatively modest lifestyle."

"Then what is it?"

Jennifer sat back in her chair and sipped her tea. She stared off into the fire. "It is many things, Jolene, that keep me there. I am very concerned about what Father would do if I left. He has been morose since Jillian left to live with Julia, and Mother is a constant trial for him. I feel terribly guilty because Jeffrey and Mother think I canceled this trip, and I asked Father to let them know when I don't come home this evening that I have come away to see you."

"And they will blame Father in some way. I didn't know you had planned on canceling this trip."

"The Morgans' gala is this week and Jeffrey had already replied that we would be there. He was angry that I would not cancel the trip and angrier still that I denied his wishes in front of Mother and Father."

"What prompted him to think you had canceled this trip then?"

Jennifer turned away, concentrating on the embroidered doilies on the arms of her chair. "I said as much to appease him. I do hate to be the source of conflict, but now it seems I have created more."

Chapter Five

ZEB ARRIVED HOME ON SEVENTEENTH Street after seven in the evening via a carriage for hire outside the offices that Max had leased for his staff. He was not sure if he'd ever been so exhausted in his entire life, meeting the staff, assessing his duties and responsibilities, and making himself familiar with the current Senate business, mostly involving monetary policy and proposals for a central U.S. bank. The day had begun before dawn and he had several early meetings to prepare for for the next day, but Max had asked him to come for dinner.

Max said his wife was insistent that he come, and although he was not terribly fond of Jolene Shelby, he was indebted to her for setting up his household prior to his arrival, even knowing she had spent a large sum of his money without his approval. He was grateful though, especially after having a taste of the pace that would have to be set in order to keep Max fully familiar with upcoming Senate business and managing the staff. Zeb knew that he would have worn his eleventh Taitlinger suit and have had no time to launder any of the previous ten let alone prepare a meal.

He arrived at Max and Jolene's home within the hour and took a long look around the massive foyer, with a winding staircase about its edge, as the butler took his coat.

"I thought I heard the door close," Max said as he came toward him, napkin in hand. "Come. We've started eating mostly because Jolene feels better if she eats at regular intervals."

Zeb had been shocked when Max told him earlier in the day that Jolene was expecting their child. He was unsure why, but he just didn't view Jolene as motherly even though she'd had quite a positive effect on Melinda. It was just then that he heard a shriek from the landing above. He looked up to see Melinda racing down the steps. She skidded to a stop just in front of him.

Zeb took off his hat and made a formal bow. "Miss Melinda Shelby. I do declare you are the most lovely young lady I have ever met."

Melinda curtsied and giggled and then launched herself into his arms. "I've missed you!"

"Me, too," he said and kissed her hair. "Have you had your dinner?"

"I ate earlier with Miss Burberry," she said.

"Zeb hasn't eaten all day, Melinda," Max said. "We're going to get some food in his belly before he faints. Hurry along now. It's near your bedtime. Your mother and I will check in on you later."

Melinda went up the steps, waving to him at every landing, until she disappeared above. "I was concerned she wouldn't care for city living, having grown up at the Hacienda, but she seems very happy," Zeb said. "I miss her."

"She misses you," Max said, and steered him down a long hall to an open set of double doors, where soft light spilled into the hallway.

Zeb walked into the dining room, knowing at first glance that it was large and elegant, nothing like the alcove where he and Max had grabbed their meals at the Hacienda when not eating in the kitchen. In his peripheral vision, he saw Jolene rise from her place and walk toward him. But his eyes, his focus, had been arrested by a woman seated directly across from the chair a servant now held for him to be seated in. Jennifer Crawford.

They stared at each other, for some long moments, Zeb thought, before he inclined his head and spoke her name. Her lips moved but he could not hear her whispered response. She was as stunningly beautiful and as outwardly delicate as he remembered her, with her golden hair piled casually on her head and her long lashes wafting furiously around sea-green eyes as she returned his regard.

"Miss Crawford," he repeated. "It is good to see you. You are looking very lovely."

It was then he remembered someone stood at his side. "Jolene," he said and turned then to her, taking both of her hands in his. "It is very good to see you again, too."

Jolene's eyebrows arched. "Really, Zebidiah? At first I didn't think you knew I was even in the room."

Zeb waited until Jolene was reseated and sat himself, spreading the linen napkin across his lap. He looked across the table just as Jennifer glanced at him. She quickly looked down at her plate.

"I want to thank you, Jolene, for arranging a house for me and the furnishings and the staff," he said. "I would have never had time to make all the arrangements, and I'd be sleeping on the settee in my office. Everything is in perfect order, thanks to you."

"You're welcome," Jolene replied. "I don't imagine you will be terribly pleased when the bills arrive, but I doubt I've beggared you."

"My sister nearly did that," he said, and then proceeded to tell them about his morning spent at Taitlinger's and amused them all with Mr. Taitlinger's anticipation of all of his purchases. "So I have arrived with a trunk full of suits and ties and shirts and shoes and even something called a tuxedo that Mr. Taitlinger was very excited about."

Zeb looked across the table at Jennifer, who was smiling at him and at his story. She took his breath away. When their eyes met, her laughter faded, and her cheeks went pink as he stared at her, unable to break himself away from the picture she made.

"What did you think of your first day in the Capital?" Max asked.

Zeb relaxed after his initial shock at seeing Jennifer and he and Max chatted about the day until Jolene cleared her throat and stood. Zeb and Max stood as well.

"Why don't you take Zebidiah to the front parlor, Jennifer? Dessert and cordials will be served while Maximillian and I check in on Melinda."

Max met Jolene at the door, leaving Jennifer and him alone. "May I escort you to the parlor?" he asked.

* * *

Jennifer rose and made her way to the door of the dining room, and Zebidiah followed. She knew that at some point she would be together with him while she visited Max and Jolene, but she was not prepared for seeing him this way, in an intimate setting, in his dress clothes and looking handsome and civilized. And now, alone together. She was still unable to stop her cheeks from reddening when she thought about him, and worse still, seeing him, she recalled the embarrassing scene in the bunkhouse at the Hacienda.

Zebidiah followed one step behind and just to her left. He didn't touch her in any way or even offer his arm, but she could *feel* him up and down her side as if he were tightly up against her as she escorted him down the carpeted hallway. The parlor door was open, and household staff were stoking the fire, attending the lamps, and laying out pastries and desserts, all quietly leaving when Jennifer entered the room. There was a coffee and tea tray on the cart, and she walked to it immediately.

"Coffee, Mr. Moran?"

"Zeb or Zebidiah, please," he said. "Coffee would suit me, Miss Crawford."

Jennifer served his coffee, poured herself tea, and sat in a chair near the fire, across from the brocade couch.

"May I get you some dessert, Miss Crawford?"

"No. Thank you. And you must call me Jennifer," she said as she sipped her tea, concentrating on the delicate flowered pattern of the china saucer.

Zeb Moran was all that was masculinity even when deathly ill, she thought, recalling him stretched out on a bunkhouse bed at The Hacienda. She had just arrived at Jolene and Max's ranch, having survived her maid leaving her to fend for herself as soon as someone mentioned the influenza at the Dallas train station, and the driver it had taken her hours to hire leaving her in the middle of the great open prairie, without a house or a person within sight. She'd seen a rider coming to her across the grasslands, as she sat on her overturned trunk, and had sent a terrified prayer to her maker that she would survive the encounter. It had been Max, thankfully, returning home from Houston on horseback as soon as he'd heard the influenza had hit the Hacienda. He'd hauled her up before him on his massive horse and continued on to find his ranch in disrepair, his staff exhausted or ill, and his daughter on her deathbed.

Jennifer had hurried to help Jolene, who was barely standing as she nursed Melinda. When the child's fever broke, Max asked Jennifer to check on those who were still sick or recovering in the bunkhouse, especially his ranch manager, while he tended his wife and daughter. And that is when she saw Zeb Moran for the first time, finding him alone and thrashing with fever, sweat-soaked and pale. She'd wiped his face and arms with cool water and changed the top sheet and blankets covering him. When he finally settled into a quiet sleep, Jennifer stepped to the window, unbuttoned her blouse, and removed it.

It had been just five days prior that she stood alone with Jeffrey in a small, rarely used room near the front entrance of Willow Tree. Her bags and trunks were being loaded onto a carriage, and her mother encouraged Jeffrey to say his good-byes to her in private. She was annoyed with her mother for suggesting such a thing, but excited as well. She and Jeffrey had been seeing each other on a regular basis and she was flattered with the attentions of such a handsome, charming man who was the favorite of every Boston debutante. She was wondering if he would kiss her, her stomach fluttering, and hoping he would. She remembered smiling up at him and sobering quickly at the look on his face.

"Jeffrey? What is wrong?" she asked.

"Wrong? What is wrong, Jennifer? You are leaving Boston when I have expressly told you it would displease me."

"But we discussed this all days ago and I thought—" Jennifer said before crumbling to the floor.

She'd never experienced pain of that intensity and struggled to breathe, finally giving into panic in a faint. She'd awakened in Jeffrey's arms as he patted her face with a hanky.

"What happened?" she whispered.

"Oh, my dear Jennifer," Jeffrey said as he kissed her forehead. "I am so very sorry to have to punish you, but you must learn to obey me. It is the nature of the relationship between men and women."

Jennifer had been confused, wondering if she'd misheard his speech in the midst of the relentless pain in her side. He had stood abruptly, pulling her to her feet, leaving her nauseous and groaning.

"*Shush*," he said. "Certainly you do not want the servants to see you in such a state. Straighten your back, Jennifer. You must hurry or you will miss your train."

She had let him lead her out to the entranceway, her hand on his arm. She remembered being unsteady on her feet and their butler, Bellings, looking at her strangely. Jeffrey had led her to the waiting carriage and kissed her on the lips softly, staring into her eyes and announcing to all that he would be counting the days until her return, and then had whispered in her ear that he was very, very sorry that she was in pain. Had begged her to believe that he didn't mean to hurt her, that she was the love of his life, but she'd best be home on the appointed day or he could not guarantee his behavior.

The door had closed on the carriage and then she did vomit, and the maid accompanying her because Eliza had been ill, a silly girl, had merely stared at the remnants of Jennifer's breakfast on the floor of the carriage, refusing to clean it up. Jennifer had pondered many times since that morning why she did not just cry out for her father or even to Bellings. Even as weak as her father sometimes was and Bellings just a servant, neither would have let her be assaulted in such a way. But she hadn't cried out. Nor had she told anyone what had happened until she'd returned from Texas and told Eliza. Much of it had seemed unreal, and she'd wondered who would believe her. She'd even let herself think it hadn't really happened until she'd taken a particularly deep breath and dealt with the ensuing pain.

Jennifer turned her head, looking out the long window of Jolene's home to the wintered gardens, and envisioned herself unbuttoning her blouse that night in the bunkhouse, slowly pulling her chemise out of the waistband of her traveling skirts and lifting it up and over her breast, to see if the massive bruises she'd seen in the mirror on the train had faded at all, touching the center of the yellow and black flesh and drawing a deep painful breath as she did. That is when she'd realized Zebidiah Moran *was no longer* fevered and sickly but awake and staring at her in such a way as to make her shiver. Jennifer looked up to find him staring at her now, realizing that she'd spent minutes, maybe five or more, remembering and reliving those horrid days.

"Are you unwell, Jennifer?" he asked quietly. "You are peaked and you cried out."

"I am fine," she said. "Thank you for asking."

He narrowed his eyes, holding her gaze. "I didn't ask that as a pleasantry. I saw your side that night in the bunkhouse, no matter how much you deny it. I saw the bruises and heard your cry of pain when you touched them. Has he hit you again?"

She swallowed and looked away. "Whatever are you talking about?"

"I am talking about the fact that someone hit you hard enough to bruise you and maybe even break a rib. I am worried it has happened again."

"Mr. Moran. Please do not be so familiar when speaking to me. Gentlemen do not bring up such a subject, especially over a lady's objection."

"Bullshit," he said. "Whoever the *gentleman* was that hit you was more than familiar."

She looked down. "I do not need to be harassed."

"Is it your father, Jennifer?" he asked. "Has your father hit you?"

"How dare you? How dare you imply that my father would ever lay a hand on my person," she hissed as she leaned forward in her chair.

"How are the cakes, Jennifer?" Jolene said from the doorway, Max just behind her.

"I do not know," she replied, and looked up with a quick smile. "Dinner was so delicious I haven't room for one more morsel. Wouldn't you agree, Mr. Moran?"

"Yes," he said, and stood. "It has been a lovely evening, especially becoming reacquainted with your sister, Jolene, but I have a very early day tomorrow and will make my good-byes now. Thank you for having me."

"You'll be a guest here often, I imagine," Jolene said. "There will be no need to stand on formality here any more than there was at the Hacienda."

"And you shouldn't find me wandering around the Capital in chaps, boots, spurs, and a layer of Texas dirt, so there'll be no need for you to remind me of the correct dinner attire."

Max laughed, and Jolene smiled a wry smile. "Let's hope not, Zebidiah. We can thank your sister for that, I suppose."

Zeb turned to Jennifer. "It's been very good seeing you again."

She smiled. "And you as well."

"I'll see you out, Zeb," Max said, and the two men left the room.

"It is very late and I am—" Jennifer began.

"What is this about Father hitting you? Why did Zebidiah ask you that?" Jolene demanded.

"I don't know what you're talking about," Jennifer said.

"When I came in the room you were very upset and said something about Father laying a hand on you. What is going on, Jennifer?"

Jennifer smiled and kissed her sister's cheek. "You are imaging things, Jolene. I am off to bed."

Jennifer climbed the steps to her room weary and furious that Zeb Moran had nearly given her away, and as equally confused as to why she cared if he did. She'd intended to tell Jolene, hadn't she? But Jolene was expecting and Max was very busy. She would not interrupt their lives with this small matter. Jeffrey Rothchild was gone from her life and most likely charming some other unfortunate young lady at this very moment.

* * *

"I still cannot believe we are finally here," Julia Crawford Shelling said to her sisters, now that she was settled in Jolene's sitting room after arriving from South Dakota late in the morning. "Traveling with children can be an adventure."

"I'm sure it can," Jolene agreed. "But I am very, very glad you made the trip. It means quite a bit to me and Maximillian."

"Jillian seems to be doing very well, especially considering she is fifteen years old," Jennifer said. "I did not think it was possible for her to be more beautiful than she was as a child, but she is. She is lovely."

"Jake says he is dreading when young men begin to come around," Julia said with a laugh. "He will be standing on the porch with a shotgun much of the time."

"Maximillian will be the same with Melinda. Perhaps that is why he and Jake seemed to get along well right away. They are together in Maximillian's study now with trays of food and coffee," Jolene said.

"Thank you so much for arranging extra staff to take care of Jacob and Mary Lou, Jolene," Julia said. "I have help with laundry and cleaning at home, but otherwise I am with the children all the time. Which I love, of course, and Jillian does help, but this is a rare treat and I am going to enjoy the peace while I can!"

"Melinda and Jillian seem to be enjoying each other's company," Jennifer observed. "I saw them in Melinda's room, their heads bent over a book."

"This is good for them both, I believe," Jolene replied. "Perhaps they will begin writing to each other."

Jennifer watched Jolene and Julia smile at each other, and it was astonishing considering their shared past. Jennifer was glad that they seemed to have let their hurts and agonies go and were now able to be happy for each other.

"Someone has to tell me—what is going on with Mother and Father?" Julia asked, then turned to Jennifer.

"Your last letter said that Mother wasn't feeling well. What is it?"

"I don't know. But I know of two times that she has been in so much pain that she has been bent over at the waist."

"What does Father say?" Jolene asked.

"Nothing. He said he does not know anything and will not press Mildred for details."

"Mildred would never reveal any information. She is completely loyal to Mother," Jolene said and took a deep breath. "As much as I dislike the idea, I'm afraid I need to go to Boston."

"Really, Jolene? You will go back?" Julia asked.

Jolene nodded. "Maximillian's family is in Boston, and his father is not doing well according to his sister Eugenia's letters. I know he is worried about him and I want to meet them both, and Melinda has not seen her grandparents since she was very small. And now Mother is ill and Jennifer is concerned for Father. I feel I must go."

Julia's eyes filled with tears. "I cannot. I cannot go."

"Then you must not," Jolene reassured. "It would be a difficult enough time without forcing your husband and children to be subject to Mother's machinations. I will settle Melinda at her grandmother's or her aunt's and stay at Willow Tree. What do you think, Jennifer?"

Jennifer stared at Jolene in shock. She did not believe either of her sisters would voluntarily go back to Willow

Tree. "But why Jolene? There will be nothing but heartache and anger."

"Perhaps. But maybe it is time for some honesty. I wish to see how Mother fares, and I realize I am missing my own father after being so worried about Maximillian's."

"Maybe I will begin writing Father. He has written me recently to apologize, and on several other occasions as well. I miss him dreadfully, too, even after all the troubles he caused Jake and me," Julia said, and wiped her eyes. "I cannot say the same of Mother. I am sorry to say I hope I never see her again."

"It is understandable," Jennifer said. "I will convey your regards to Father, Julia. He wanted me to tell you how sorry he was to not be able to make this trip. That he is very proud of Max and Jolene and that he misses you and would have wanted to apologize in person and meet his grandchildren. I think he particularly wanted to see Jillian again."

Chapter Six

"I HAVE NOT DANCED LIKE this in ages!" Julia said to her husband, Jake, and Jennifer as they stood to the side of the ballroom on the evening of Max's swearing in.

"And you look as pretty as a picture in that new dress," Jake replied, and dropped a kiss on his wife's cheek.

"We had an exceptionally enjoyable time at Jolene's dressmaker," Jennifer confessed with a smile. "The seamstress must have thought us ridiculous with all of our laughter and giggling."

Jennifer looked around at the ballroom as she tapped her foot to the music. Two-story windows graced one entire side, with layers of cascading draperies in yellow and blue. Dozens and dozens of couples twirled their way around the gleaming wood floors to the sounds of the orchestra's music. She was wearing a new dark red gown with a daringly low neckline and lace sleeves, and enjoying herself immensely at the celebration ball for Max's election. She knew very few guests and would never remember all of the men and women Jolene had introduced her to, but she would remember the admiring gazes from some of the young men she'd been introduced to. She'd been asked to dance every dance so far.

"Good evening, Jennifer," Zeb Moran said just as a waltz was forming. "May I have this dance?"

All the good humor and gayness drained from Jennifer's face as she was reminded of her shame, and her secrets. She had tried not to let herself think of Zeb, even though she compared all of the men she met that evening to him and found them lacking. Not every young man could be thin-hipped and broad shouldered like Zeb, she said to herself. Not many men had his light brown hair that melted to blond at the crown or pale blue eyes that focused completely on her as he spoke.

"Yes, of course," she replied, and handed her glass of lemonade to Julia, who winked at her.

Zeb was a good dancer, and just the right height for her, swinging her around the dance floor with ease, maneuvering them through the throng and past older sedate couples who were moving slowly, without taking his eyes off of her.

"Are you enjoying Washington?" she asked.

"I miss Texas, but yes, I am enjoying Washington. I have the greatest regards for your brother-in-law, and am honored to serve him."

"I imagine you are very good at your work."

"I like to think so, but . . ."

He stopped midsentence as he pulled her close to his chest as a very large man stumbled by, knocking other dancers out of the way.

"What a clumsy fool!" Zeb groused, and released her to her natural dance position. "Too much whiskey, I'd say."

Jennifer took short breaths and concentrated on not fainting. Zeb had pulled her close by reaching around her and grabbing her by her side, exactly where Jeffrey had hit her the night at the theatre. It was all she could do not to cry out, but even still she winced in pain. Within moments, she found herself whisked through double doors and on to the side patio. Zeb immediately took off his jacket, set it about her shoulders, and led her to a stone bench.

"I am so terribly sorry, Jennifer," he said as he knelt before her. "I've hurt you. Tell me what I can do?"

She shook her head. "I will be fine. I just need a moment to catch my breath."

"Did I step on your foot? I'm a clumsy oaf in these new boots and was in a hurry to get you out of the way of that lumbering drunk."

"You did not step on my foot, Zeb," she said, and willed herself to smile. "It is nothing."

He stared at her. "Did I hurt you when I pulled you out of the way? When I touched you here?" he asked and gently reached under her arm.

She took in a quick, halting breath as his finger touched her ribs and closed her eyes.

He picked up her hands from her lap and held them in a loose grip. "Easy," he whispered. "Take your time and breathe through the pain. Easy."

Jennifer concentrated on the quiet soothing rhythm of his voice, taking shallow breaths and allowing her racing heart to slow. "Is this how you calm horses when they are agitated?"

Zeb chuckled softly. "It is, but I'd never in a lifetime compare you to a mare."

"I am glad to hear that," she said, finally opening her eyes and seeing that his face was inches from hers.

"How do you know how I talk to horses?"

"I watched you from my room at the Hacienda when you were in the corral. I saw you get close to a bucking, agitated horse and rub its head and soon the horse was calm and putting its nose in your palm."

"I'm flattered you paid such close attention."

Jennifer's breathing quickened but not from pain. His eyes had dropped to her lips as they parted, allowing her to survey his face, his tan skin against the white of his collar, and the gold flecks in the blue of his eyes. She smelled shaving soap and lifted her hand to his cheek. He sucked in a breath.

"How did you chip your tooth?" she asked as she ran her thumb over his lower lip. He smiled.

"Fistfighting," he said, bringing his eyes to hers. "I was a hellion."

She met his gaze, feeling the heat of his look down to the pit of her stomach, and lower. She licked her lips, and Zeb stood abruptly.

"Would you like to go to your rooms? Are you able to walk?" he asked.

"Just take me inside," she said, recovering her composure, and realizing how very close she had come to kissing him. She nearly touched her lips to his! And she had touched his lip with her thumb and found it warm and soft as compared to the bristles of his beard on his cheeks. *Zeb Moran is all that is solid and right*, she thought to herself, unbidden.

* * *

Jennifer stopped just before stepping inside the ballroom, and turned to him. "You have been very kind and have asked me no questions. Thank you."

"You're welcome," he replied, gazing down at her. Whatever her reasons, be they right or wrong, she was bearing her burdens alone, and he admired her strength. He'd nearly kissed her as she sat on the stone bench and laid her hand on his cheek. It had taken all his considerable discipline to remember this woman was in pain and bearing some hidden terrors, and he had no right to upset her fragile equilibrium. If she chose to tell him, he would listen patiently, and be her champion if she asked. But then it occurred to him that the bruising he'd seen in the moonlight at the Hacienda months ago would have likely faded. Meaning she had been hit again. How could he allow it to continue?

"Why don't we find the punch bowl and a place to sit down?" he asked.

Zeb seated her at one of the small tables in the anteroom where uniformed staff were serving lemonade and stronger spirits.

"How have you found Washington?" he asked after being served cold drinks.

"Max took Melinda and me to the Capitol building and to some other sites nearby. I find the history of the city very interesting. And I've accompanied Jolene, and my sister Julia, and her daughter Jillian, now that they have arrived, and Jolene's sister-in-law Eugenia, to some of the famous shops."

"I am glad you are enjoying yourself. I wonder how Jolene had the time to arrange my house and its furnishings and staff with the festivities she needed to supervise here, but I have seen my sister in action managing my father's household and our family's obligations at church and in the community. I stay out of her way unless I am given a direct order," Zeb added with a smile.

"Jolene is very good at all that. I am not, and thankfully am not called upon to do it often."

Zeb laughed. "What are your interests? Do you volunteer with a hospital or your church as so many young ladies do?"

"I do not."

"Do you enjoy music, perhaps play an instrument?"

"No."

He wondered if the pain in her side had returned as she was sitting very still and looking at her hands where they held a glass of lemonade. He was content to be quiet with her, though, even in the bustle of the festivities all around them. He realized he would perhaps be content with her anywhere. She looked up at him then, her cheeks flushed.

"I go to my family's business four days a week, the Crawford Bank that is, and greet important customers as they arrive for appointments with my father and with vice presidents of the bank," Jennifer said, and then squared her shoulders, looking at him directly. "And I unravel difficult accounts that cannot be balanced by the clerks. I have an assistant, O'Brien, and we tally rows and sheets of figures, looking for errors."

"You're an accountant?"

"I don't know. I've never called myself that. I go to the bank to help my father."

"I am in awe, Jennifer. I cannot remember or add five numbers in a row, and you do pages of them in your head?"

"We also use a new addition machine from the Burroughs Company. It's very exciting actually. I can tally . . . oh, do forgive me, I don't mean to prattle on."

Zeb had never seen Jennifer Crawford as animated and engaged as she was when she began to talk about her work. She was staring at him now with pleading eyes, as if starved to have someone listen to her. He shook his head and reached for her hands. "Please, do go on. I'm very interested. I want to hear about what you do."

Jennifer told him more about the new addition machine and how she used it to spot errors. She said numbers were natural for her and sometimes she knew instinctively where to uncover mathematical mistakes within a complicated portfolio, and that seeing pages and pages of figures was exciting to her. Zeb was fascinated and surprised; if he were truthful, he would have never guessed Jennifer Crawford had such a hidden passion.

"I was at the top of my graduating class for mathematics at the Ramsey School when I finished my studies there. Oh, dear, I did not mean to be a braggart," she said finally, as a blush climbed her face. "I really have gone on and on. They are serving supper and I have kept us back."

"I could always tell you were very clever, Jennifer, but I had no idea you were brilliant. I should have known, though. As my mother would often say when she was alive, 'still waters run deep.' Let us go into supper now because everyone else will be seated and I can arrive with the most beautiful and the most talented lady at the ball on my arm. It will do my ego good."

She laughed. A light, musical sound free from worry and concern. "You are a flatterer, Zebidiah Moran."

I am a man falling for a woman, he thought.

* * *

"Zebidiah Moran is very handsome, and he is clearly very interested in you. He couldn't take his eyes off of you last night," Julia said to Jennifer as Eliza fixed her hair in her sleeping room the morning following the ball.

"He is very handsome," Jennifer conceded.

"And I saw that you were whisked out the door of the ballroom and gone for ten minutes or more. Was he stealing a kiss?"

"He . . . stepped on my toes and just took me outside to catch my breath."

"*Hmmm*," Julia said as she turned to the door from where she sat on Jennifer's bed. "Whatever is that noise? Is that Max shouting?"

"I think it is."

"How peculiar!"

Julia and Jennifer stepped into the hallway and saw Max striding toward them. He stopped, turned back to the closed door of his wife's room, and shouted, "This is not over, Jolene Crawford Shelby! By damn, it is not over." He turned to Julia and Jennifer. "Good morning, ladies, and pardon my coarse language. I'm sorry you have to witness your sister and me have one of our rare tiffs, but she can be the most stubborn, inflexible woman and on this subject, I don't intend to give in!"

Max stomped by and Julia and Jennifer hurried down the hallway to Jolene's rooms.

"Whatever is going on, Jolene?" Julia asked once inside. "Max is furious!"

Jolene was stretched out on a settee near the window, wearing a voluminous white silk robe embroidered with tiny pink roses and matching slippers. She shrugged. "Maximillian is unhappy I am going to Boston. He *forbade* it, he said. How ridiculous he is being all because I am expecting."

Julia laughed.

"Perhaps you should not go, Jolene. Max is very angry," Jennifer cautioned.

"And his anger will be dealt with by him, not I," she said. "I told him that your maid would be with us and if he wanted to send a manservant for the train trip, I would allow it to ease his worries."

All three women turned when they heard doors slam from somewhere belowstairs.

"I don't think that eased his worries," Julia said.

Jolene raised her brows. "I won't be bullied. I'm an adult woman in 1893 with the intelligence and wherewithal to board a train and arrive unscathed in the city of Boston, the city I grew up in and still know intimately. And anyway, Father will send a carriage to the station, so there would be no concerns about my safety or how we would get around."

Jolene's bedroom door banged open and Julia and Jennifer turned with a start. Max stood there, red-faced and angry.

"I can't take the worry, Jolene," he shouted. "I can't take it. If you insist on this, I will excuse myself from my Senate duties and escort you."

"You would miss all the important votes that you have been working so diligently on? Why can't a manservant accompany us? It would not be unusual, and he could report back to you the following day that we had arrived and that he had turned his guardianship of us over to my father."

"I can't trust just anyone with you, and the baby, and Melinda, and Jennifer, too," Max insisted, looking suddenly arrested and hurrying from the room.

Jolene picked at her robe and looked at her sisters. "Marriage can be a trial, especially if one is in love with one's husband. Maximillian shouts and slams doors to display his displeasure. I tell him he is far too earthy to be a real gentleman."

"And what does he say to that?" Julia asked.

"He says little, but I'm certain you know, Julia," Jolene said with a throaty laugh, "there is something to be said about an earthy man in the bedroom."

"Jolene!" Julia said, but covered her mouth to stifle a laugh.

"I hate to see Max upset, Jolene," Jennifer said. "You must wait and come another time when Max can come with you. He is so worried about you!"

"Sometimes it's best to have a conversation with those we love, even if it becomes loud or angry," Julia said and wandered to the window. "Imagine how much less pain there would have been in the long term for our family if I'd been honest with Jolene about Turner and me right away?"

"You were seventeen years old, Julia, and your mother, our mother, directed you to do what you did. There is no shock or shame in doing as you'd been told," Jolene said.

"Perhaps we shouldn't discuss this." Jennifer's face reddened. How could her sisters be so casual about the events that tore their family apart? It was so much easier to avoid arguments and these painful issues, and so much better when an issue seemed to go away for having ignored it, rather than focusing endlessly on things others were saying or doing. But *did* the unpleasantness ever go away?

Jolene looked at Jennifer and tilted her head as if observing something new about her sister. "I believe you've learned an unfortunate lesson at Mother's hands. You do not like confrontation and will go out of your way to avoid it. I am the same to some degree but have been able to overcome it."

"I avoided everything so much I boarded a train to marry a man I'd never met," Julia added, and turned. "It is a hard habit to break, Jennifer. But you must."

"I don't know what you mean," Jennifer replied. Jolene was staring at her and Julia was looking at her with pity. She faced accounting problems head-on, but what of the troubles in her life?

* * *

Jennifer was seated in the front parlor with her sisters and Julia's husband, Jake, discussing their museum outing of that afternoon.

"The best part of the day was the meal," Jake declared.

"Oh, Jake," Julia said with a laugh. "You would say that. Can you imagine how excited your sisters, Flossie and Gloria, would be to see all those beautiful paintings? In a few years, when the children are older, I will bring them here on the train. What do you think, Jake?"

Jake smiled at his wife. "I think that once you get an idea in your head, you hang on to it like a dog with a bone. Boarding in this town would be plenty expensive, though, if the prices I saw on that restaurant menu are typical."

"You and your sisters and brothers-in-law and their children would be more than welcome to stay here if you decide to come," Jolene said to Jake. "Maximillian wouldn't hear of allowing our family to stay at a hotel."

"What wouldn't I allow?" Max asked as he came into the room, Zebidiah following him.

Jolene grasped Max's hand and tilted her cheek up for a kiss. "Julia would like to bring her sisters-in-law to Washington to see the museums and other sites. I told them you would never allow them to stay at a hotel and that we would be happy to have them here."

Max kissed Jolene's cheek and hand and turned to Jake. "Your family is welcome to stay anytime."

"You seem to be in a better mood than you were this morning, Maximillian. How did things go at the Senate?" Jolene asked.

"The Senate is full of backstabbing sycophants without the wherewithal to form an educated opinion," Max said, and smiled. "My problems of early this morning, though, relating to my beautiful wife who does not always, if ever, mind her husband, are solved for all concerned."

Jolene raised her brows. "Really, Maximillian? Do tell."

Max put his arm around Zeb and pulled him forward. "Zeb is going to accompany you to Boston and stay until you and Melinda are ready to come home. What do you think of that?"

"I think Zebidiah's considerable talents will be wasted and that you need him for important government business," Jolene said.

Max shook his head. "He is the only man I trust to take care of you, other than my newly made friend and relative, Jake, who has women and children of his own to guard, and Eugenia's husband, Calvin." He knelt down in front of Jolene's chair and clasped her hands. "There are threats made every day, according to what the Pinkerton agent told us. To ourselves and to our families, and I take them seriously."

"Poor Zebidiah. What does he have to say about this arrangement?" Jolene asked.

"I serve at the senator's pleasure," Zeb replied. "If this is how I can best be of service, than I am happy to comply."

Everyone stood as dinner was announced, but Jennifer could not think of food or the lovely time she'd had with Jolene, Melinda, and Julia and her family that afternoon. She'd been thinking about the precious memories she would have of the laughter and the lightheartedness she'd felt that day, only wishing her father was with them. But then Max announced that Zeb would be traveling with them to Boston. The idea of Jolene and Mother under the same roof again had left her sleepless with worry, but now, with the chance that Mother would be introduced to Zeb, she could barely breathe! She locked arms with Jolene.

"This is unwise," she whispered to her sister. "What if Mother were to meet Zeb? She would be rude and cruel."

Jolene looked at her and stopped them in the long hallway before they followed the others to the dining room. "Mother will certainly meet Zebidiah as he will be staying at Willow Tree."

"Oh, no! He must not. Mother will not like it, and you know how she can be. I can't even imagine what she'll say to . . ." she trailed off and looked at her hands folded at her waist.

"Are you concerned about Mother's behavior toward me?" She led Jennifer to a settee. "We are not doing anything untoward. I am a married daughter visiting her mother and father and I will have a trusted escort, as my husband's profession can attract an undesirable element. There is nothing to be ashamed about. Nothing strange unless you allow Mother's influences to rule you. Do you really think Father would keep me from staying at Willow Tree?"

Jennifer shook her head. "No. I'm certain Father misses you and Julia, and Jillian, too, and will be very happy for you to stay."

"Then you must not let Mother set the tone for this visit. We will manage Mother together, find out more about her illness, and spend time with our father. I intend to send out a letter to him tomorrow. Come. Come and eat and try to relax. Nothing dreadful will happen. I promise."

Chapter Seven

JENNIFER AND JOLENE SAT TOGETHER on a plush sofa talking quietly in the private car of the train they were taking to Boston. Zeb sat on a bench seat near the opposite window with Melinda, who was giving him a running narrative of everything she saw as she looked through the glass at the landscape as it went by. Jennifer was white-faced, distracted, and looked ill, Zeb thought, with even more of her usual reticence. Jolene had barely left her side, and he wondered if she knew what troubled Jennifer. He doubted it though. If Jolene knew, then Max would know and that would mean Max would be on this train to Boston intent on making sure Jennifer's tormentor was gone from her life permanently.

"You are not paying any attention to me," Melinda said.

"That is not true," he replied. "You just told me you counted twenty cows in the last pasture before it was out of sight."

Melinda giggled. "It was thirty goats, but you were very close."

"Miss Burberry?" Jolene said to the middle-aged woman seated at one end of the car, book in hand. "Would you take Melinda to the dining car? There is a table in my name for five. You may order drinks and soup if you would like. We will join you in a few minutes."

"Certainly ma'am," Miss Burberry said and rose, waiting for Melinda to follow her.

"What are you going to talk about Mother?" Melinda asked. "That is why you are asking us to leave, am I right? I am nearly thirteen. I don't know why I can't stay."

"You may not stay because I have requested privacy with your Aunt Jennifer and Mr. Moran," Jolene said.

"Come along, Melinda," Miss Burberry said. "We will order lemonade or cold tea and pretend we are grand ladies."

Jolene waited until the train car door latched firmly and looked at Zeb. "Our family home, Willow Tree, is not always a comfortable place to be, mostly because of our mother."

Jennifer stood and huffed a breath. "We shouldn't be talking about this. Perhaps he should be staying at a hotel."

"If you would prefer I stay at a hotel, I will be glad to," Zeb said.

"Jennifer, please sit down. No. I don't believe you should stay at a hotel, and I don't believe Maximillian would be happy if you did. He was very specific in his instructions, was he not?"

"Very specific. But I've no wish to upset your sister."

Jennifer seated herself at the end of the sofa and Jolene rose and sat down beside her. She picked up Jennifer's hand and squeezed it. "Our mother is a very unhappy person. She has been known to be cruel and malicious, and now she is unwell. Our father loves her even with all of that, and tries to please her, and maintain peace. It is difficult. Jennifer is, and I am as well, I suppose, embarrassed that you may be subject to her insults. I will introduce Melinda to her and then take her to stay with Maximillian's sister and her husband. I do not want her subject to Mother's rants."

Jennifer wiped her eyes. "She will undoubtedly be mean to you, too, Jolene. She said you and Julia are dead to her."

"I did not acquiesce to her demands." Jolene turned to Zeb. "My husband trusts you implicitly and that is why he sent you on this trip with us. I am asking for Jennifer's and my sake that you do not repeat any of what you see and hear. I have consulted physicians and am convinced my mother has a mental illness above and beyond the physical illness that Jennifer has reported to us."

Jennifer was crying softly and covered her face with her hand. Jolene was staring at him. "I would never repeat anything I heard or saw. It is not my place to carry tales other than to Max in regards to your safety. My father is . . . does not pay attention to the world around him. He is a professor and he barricades himself in his study or at his university office. He is not actively cruel but neglectful of those dependent on him. My mother, when she lived, maintained peace in our family. I am able to navigate awkward situations when it is called for."

"Of course you are. That is why Maximillian is dependent on your help with his fellow senators."

Jolene stood, gave him a pointed look, and started to the door. "Join us for lunch when you are ready."

"I am sorry about your mother," Jennifer said after Jolene had gone from their train car.

"Thank you," Zeb said, and knelt in front of her. "Please do not be upset or worried for me. Have you heard the children's rhyme? 'Sticks and stones may break my bones but words will never harm me'?"

"I have not," she said. "But I should take it to heart, shouldn't I? I worry excessively about things I can do nothing about."

"You do not worry when confronted with an accounting problem, do you?"

"Well, no. It is in my power to solve those problems. Mother is not one of those problems."

"I believe you can do whatever it is you set your mind to. Your father depends on you to solve the most difficult issues at your family's business. For all your beauty and style, you were never afraid to work hard. I watched you while you were at the Hacienda helping with all the influenza patients, myself included. And now you are facing problems at home that seem insurmountable, and some may be dangerous, and yet you manage it alone."

Perhaps this was the time to tell Zeb why her ribs were tender. He was the only man, the only person really, to recognize her in her own right. She was not an appendage in his eyes, rather fully formed as her own person. He had said it to her, just then, and his words, as she repeated them in her head, were more meaningful and dear than anything anyone else had ever said to her. She was not a sister or daughter to him. She was Jennifer Crawford, with her own hopes and dreams and strengths understood. She was suddenly glad of his company and the extended time she would have getting to know him.

"You are a very perceptive man, and you are too kind. But I confess my greatest concern now is that we may miss luncheon."

He rose and held out his hand to help her from her seat. "You have read my mind or heard my stomach churning. We do not want to miss our meal."

* * *

"What is that ungodly racket?" Jane Crawford said as she came down the grand staircase at Willow Tree.

"Look who is home, Jane," William Crawford said to his wife. "Jennifer is back, and Jolene is visiting, too, and has brought guests."

Father looks terrified, Jennifer thought to herself. *How ridiculous! In his own home!* His behavior would have been normal for her as well had she not escaped for the past month. She was determined to not let Mother intimidate her or belittle her. She'd become accustomed to being treated kindly and with respect. She recently decided she would not go back.

"Jolene is no longer a member of this family. She can take herself and these people out of my house at once."

Jennifer pulled off her gloves and handed them to Bellings as she walked to her mother and kissed her cheek. "How absurd you are being, Mother! Jolene is your daughter just as I am and Julia is. And she has brought her daughter, Melinda. Come here, Melinda, and meet your grandmother."

"I am not—" Jane began.

"You will not say one nasty word to this child. She has done nothing to you," Jennifer whispered as she leaned close. Her mother turned her head sharply and eyed her.

"Hello. It is nice to meet you," Melinda said to Jane and then looked at Jennifer.

Jennifer smiled even as her stomach rolled while waiting for her mother to respond.

But Jane merely nodded.

"Come along now, Melinda. I am taking you to your Aunt Eugenia and Uncle Calvin's. Your aunt wrote me that she is prepared to spoil you with new dresses and fancy dinners and that your father and I are to say nothing," Jolene said.

Jolene and Melinda went back to the carriage where Zeb waited to escort them to the Billingses'. Jennifer looked at her mother.

"You look very tired since I saw you last. How are you feeling?"

"You are home less than five minutes and are insulting me already?"

"It is not meant as an insult, Mother. I am concerned about you, as is Jolene."

"Jolene did not speak one word to me, and she has not been in this house for nearly two years!"

"What did you expect her to say, Mother? You told her she was not a member of the family and that she was to leave."

"Well," Jane said. "What is expected of *me* in light of her behavior?"

"We are glad to have you home, Jennifer," her father said as he came to stand beside her. "We have missed you."

"We are not the only ones to have missed you either. Jeffrey—" Her mother suddenly folded at the waist. "William. William. Get me to my rooms!"

"Mother!" Jennifer cried, and turned quickly to Bellings. "Fetch Dr. Roderdeck immediately and see that Mildred goes directly to Mrs. Crawford's rooms."

"No doctor!" her mother gasped as she straightened and took deep breaths.

Jennifer locked eyes with her father, and then he looked at his wife.

"Yes there will be a doctor, Jane. I will not have you suffer like this," he said.

Her mother suddenly looked old to her. Old and ill, even dressed as she was in a stylish outfit, her hair fixed and her rouge applied expertly. "Come along, Mother. I will help you to your rooms now that you have caught your breath."

"I will take care of your mother from here, Miss Crawford," Mildred, her mother's maid, said as she took her mistress's arm at the door to her rooms. "You needn't trouble yourself."

"Thank you, Mildred. But I will help you and wait with Mother until Dr. Roderdeck arrives."

"That isn't necessary, Miss Crawford. I am used to helping Mrs. Crawford."

"I am certain you are; however, it is necessary for me to stay," Jennifer said and swept past Mildred into her mother's rooms. "Let us get you changed into a dressing gown, Mother. I will wait with you until the doctor arrives."

After her mother was out of her day dress and in a gown and robe, Jennifer watched her go from the stool at her dressing table to a chair near the window, and finally pace from one end of the room to the other. "Mother. Please lie down and rest," Jennifer begged.

"I feel fine. I do not need a doctor."

Jane jumped at the knock at her door. Jennifer hurried to answer it and admitted Dr. Roderdeck to the room. "Her maid and I will wait in her dressing room while you examine her."

Jennifer sat on an overstuffed footstool while Mildred stared at her. Dr. Roderdeck knocked on the dressing room door, and Jennifer hurried to her mother's side as she lay stretched out on the bed. She was screaming.

"He is a charlatan! An imposter! He knows nothing about modern medicine! Get him out of my rooms!"

"Dr. Roderdeck, if you are done here, please come with me so that you may speak to my father. He is very worried for his wife," Jennifer said.

"Mrs. Crawford? Do you have any questions for me?" he asked.

"I will not have him telling your father his lies, Jennifer. Escort him directly out of the house."

"Rest now," Jennifer said. "I will be back to check on you shortly."

"Your wife has a tumor in her stomach area. It should be removed surgically," the doctor said once seated in William Crawford's study. "She was difficult to examine, and I don't believe she answered all my questions truthfully."

"What does that mean?" Jennifer asked.

"There is a mass, an abnormal growth, growing near or around her stomach or intestines. I cannot say if it is cancerous or not. It may be benign; however, we will not know until it is removed. It is pressing on her organs and causing her discomfort as you know."

"I doubt if Jane will agree to surgery," her father said.

"You must convince her, Father," Jennifer said. "You must."

"This mass will undoubtedly continue to grow," Dr. Roderdeck stated as he stood to leave. "And the pain will worsen."

"Mother must have this surgery. We can hardly allow her to wither away in front of us," Jennifer told her father after the door to the study had closed.

"I cannot stand seeing her in so much pain. Is there any medicine that may help her? Has he prescribed any?"

"He offered her morphine. She refused."

William Crawford stood and stared out the long window. "Your mother can be difficult," he said finally. "I do not wish to talk about her behind her back, but this ailment will only increase her anxiety and stress and may prompt unpleasant words and situations. You should prepare yourself."

"I am well aware of Mother's moods and the miserable affect they have on every member of this household, Father. Certainly you don't believe that no one noticed?"

"I will not tolerate harsh words about your mother, Jennifer."

Jennifer walked to where he stood and looked at him very directly. "Father. How can you say you will not tolerate harsh words about Mother? We know nothing else. We have lived with nothing but harsh words and manipulations from her all of our lives. I will be kind to Mother, of course, and make allowances for her physical condition, but I will not allow her to belittle me. I won't allow it anymore."

Jennifer had spoken quietly, when she wanted to scream out her frustration and anger, realizing at that moment that her father knew no other way of life, knew only his place in her mother's world and the excuses he needed to make to justify his own existence. She watched him now, as he stared at her, regret and sorrow on his face.

"I always hoped that I was able to make up for some of the excesses of your mother's personality, but it appears I have not. Have I been a fool, Jennifer?"

"No," she said, shaking her head and taking her father's hand in hers. "No, you have never been a fool. You have worked hard and made a comfortable life for all of us and been a wonderful father. You love all of your daughters, I am certain, and you love Mother very much. You've never been a fool."

William's eyes glistened. "You mother was not loved as a girl. It has continued to haunt her all these years later."

Jennifer nodded. "She is an unhappy person. Jolene believes she may be mentally unstable and has done some research on the subject."

"Mentally unstable? What has Jolene found out about this? I . . . it's just that your mother is unhappy. You must never repeat this. It would be devastating to your mother to think we thought her out of her wits. And now she is ill and in pain."

* * *

"So you have come home to beg our forgiveness and move back to Boston, Jolene?" Jane Crawford said to her daughter later that evening as the family gathered before dinner. "It is long past time."

Jolene shook her head. "I have no intentions of moving anywhere, Mother. I am here for a visit and to make myself acquainted with Maximillian's parents."

"Did Melinda get settled at her aunt's?" Jennifer asked.

"Yes. I will be dining with Calvin and Eugenia on several evenings with Maximillian's parents, as his mother entertains little these days," Jolene said, and looked at her mother. "Eugenia is Maximillian's sister and she has asked me to invite you and father to dinner at their home."

"We have no intentions of dining with those people. Would you have me muck stalls and clean the commodes?" Jane said and grimaced. "You will not be dining there, either. To think that you lower yourself to those people, Jolene. I'm ashamed."

"Mother!" Jennifer cried. "Those are Jolene and her husband's relatives."

"Jolene's husband is dead. She infected him and let him die." Jane sniffed. "And our baby as well. She let Little William die."

Jolene's face was ashen and her lips a tight thread. Jennifer touched her hand where it gripped the chair and took a deep breath. "That is enough, Mother. I will not let you upset Jolene in this way, and Father and me as well."

"And who are you to censor me? I'll not stand for such disrespect," Jane hissed.

"No more, please, Jane," William Crawford said as his wife sputtered and fidgeted in her seat.

"Good evening," Zeb called from the doorway. "I hope I'm not interrupting a family conversation."

"No. Do come in. May I serve you a whiskey or wine?" William said.

"Mother. This is Zebidiah Moran. He works for Jolene's husband and was asked to accompany us in our travels," Jennifer said.

Zeb bowed at the waist. "It is my pleasure to meet you, Mrs. Crawford." Jane said nothing, and Zeb turned to her husband. The men shook hands and Zeb accepted his tumbler of whiskey.

"I was surprised to read Jolene's letter that you would be coming with my daughters," William said. "Are you on leave from the senator's offices?"

"No, sir," Zeb said. "The senator is concerned about threats to members of Congress and their families, and insisted on an escort for his wife, daughter, and sister-in-law. He wanted to carry out the task himself but is sponsoring an important bill that is coming up for a vote very soon."

"Jennifer," Jane said. "Why is this person here with us? Have them set a place for him in the staff kitchens."

"He is here because Jolene's husband is concerned for her and he is a trusted employee and a guest of Willow Tree. Father invites bank employees to dine with us occasionally and they do not eat in the kitchens, do they?"

Jane leaned forward and winked. "Speaking of the bank, I have sent Mr. Rothchild an invitation to dine with us tomorrow evening. He is most anxious to see you, I imagine."

"Why would you do that, Mother, without consulting me?"

Jane shrugged. "He is your fiancé, Jennifer. Of course, I will invite him to dine with us. Don't be ridiculous."

Jennifer could feel her heart pounding in her chest and the blood drain from her face. How could she have thought she would so easily extract herself from this situation? She saw Zeb and her father deep in conversation and glanced at Jolene.

"Jennifer sent Mr. Rothchild a letter telling him that she no longer wished to see him," Jolene explained. "It will be an uncomfortable dinner, no doubt."

"Your father and I have given him our blessing, and everyone knows he is courting you. You are young and foolish and would have no idea how to choose the right husband. You will marry Mr. Rothchild. I believe a Christmas wedding would suit."

Jennifer stood and moved close to her mother's chair. "Do not," she whispered hoarsely, "begin planning any such event. You will be the one left looking very foolish in the eyes of Boston society."

"My sister-in-law asked me if Jennifer had set a date for her wedding to Mr. Rothchild, and I informed her that there is nothing between my sister and Mr. Rothchild so there would be no date to set," Jolene said.

"Who would your relatives tell?" Jane asked with a laugh. "The chimney sweep? They are not included in Boston society."

"Really? They are attending the Autumn Gala at the museum. Eugenia is a committee woman for that event."

Jane's mouth opened and closed. "Money-grubbers. And good society is forced to mingle with them."

Dinner was announced, and Jennifer and Jolene walked down the long hallway together. "I will continue to think of her as being mentally ill," Jolene said. "I cannot bear to think that anyone would be so cruel to their own daughters and be sane."

"What she said to you was horrible, Jolene."

"I had forgotten how uncomfortable and tense she makes even the most benign gathering. We all wait in anticipation of who she will torment. She does back down somewhat when we present a united front. She had us at a disadvantage when we were young by pitting us against each other."

"I agree," Jennifer said and recounted her conversation with their father that afternoon.

"And father is most concerned with what mother would think?" Jolene asked.

Jennifer shook her head. "No. I don't believe so. I think he has always thought we didn't notice how dreadful she could be."

"It is difficult when the foundations of all you believe to be true are shaken," Jolene said. "You have given our father much to think about."

* * *

"So, Jennifer," Jane said when the soup course was served. "The Randolphs are having a dinner dance. We must visit the dressmaker and begin looking for a new gown for you."

"I haven't received an invitation from the Randolphs," Jennifer said.

"But Mr. Rothchild has, of course, and he will escort you. No more of this silly chatter about breaking off your relationship with him. I don't imagine Jeffrey is the type of man who would expect his intended to be coy."

"I am not his intended," Jennifer replied.

Zeb watched Jennifer as her mother continued to claim that Jeffrey Rothchild was still her fiancé. Jennifer was pale and her hands shook as she reached for her wine. Her sister watched her closely and interjected when Jennifer faltered. The father sat by idly, eating his lamb and smiling occasionally in Zeb's direction. It was as if he saw or felt none of the tension between the three women. This was not the man who would be bullying Jennifer, leaving only one candidate. Jeffrey Rothchild.

"I'm going to the library to look for a book," Jennifer said after dessert and dinner were served. Her mother had declared herself exhausted and that she would be retiring to her rooms. Jolene and her father were talking quietly at one end of the dining room.

"May I join you?" he asked.

"Yes," she said, and waited for him in the hallway. "Father keeps an impeccable library. He has several first editions and buys all the latest popular works and dime novels as well. He says they are his guilty secret."

"I have been so busy reading Senate bills and the like that I haven't had time to read for pleasure," he said.

Zeb spent thirty minutes combing the books in the Crawford library. He finally settled on a collection of Thomas Jefferson's writings and a dark-looking novel from a magazine writer named Wilde. Jennifer was thumbing through a stack of books beside her on a sofa.

"Nothing caught your fancy?" he asked.

"I find most popular books to be so unrealistic they are laughable," she said, and straightened a folded page in the book she was holding. "Life is not always happy or without tragedy. And it does not always have a happy ending."

"Very true. It appears though that your sisters have found theirs."

She nodded and looked at him. "Yes they have. I am very glad for them both."

"Will you find a happy ending, do you think?" he asked.

"I don't think so," she whispered.

Zeb poured himself a bourbon from the cart stocked with crystal decanters as her response echoed in his head. She didn't hold out hope for herself from the sound of it, and that thought hit him square in the chest. What could be done to make her happy? What would he do?

"Would you care for anything to drink?" he asked.

"No, thank you. I am going to the bank tomorrow and don't want to have a fuzzy head in the morning. I've already had two glasses of wine with dinner," she said, resting her chin on her hand and staring at the dying fire.

"You'll want a clear head, I suppose, for dinner tomorrow evening with Mr. Rothchild."

She nodded.

"Your mother thinks Mr. Rothchild is your happy ending. Do you?"

Tears filled her eyes. "There would be nothing happy about a permanent association with Jeffrey Rothchild."

There was little to say after that declaration and little doubt now about who was causing this woman to cry and be terrified. Zeb looked forward to meeting Jeffrey Rothchild.

Chapter Eight

"GOOD MORNING AND WELCOME BACK," O'Brien said, and helped Jennifer off with her cloak.

"It is good to be back. I have missed my desk and my numbers," Jennifer said.

"And they have missed you. I still cannot untangle the Dorchester portfolio your father brought us shortly before you left. But I have become proficient with the new Burroughs machine!"

Jennifer smiled. "We shall take a look at it together. Have you managed to learn anything about the initials on the certificates?"

"The two signatures that were different from the four certificates signed by the one person I have figured out.

Hawkins and Marlow, both junior bookkeepers. They both work mostly for your father unless one of the vice presidents is away, and then Mr. Marlow fills in where needed."

Jennifer pulled the pins from her hat and shook the raindrops off of the hem of her skirts. She had hurried through the lobby in a rush, hoping that Jeffrey was already ensconced in his office. "I would like to begin immediately unless we have guests to entertain. And we need to find out whose initials are on the other certificates."

"Yes, ma'am. I have some ideas and will begin straightaway as we have no guests today."

Jennifer straightened her back after hours of examining documents. She requested multiple portfolios and began a rigorous comparison of the percentages charged on certificates. She found multiple other certificates charging six percent interest, but more interesting than all of that was that the final totals reflected the interest charged as five percent. She could not fathom how a figure began at one amount and ended up at another at the bottom of the tally sheet.

O'Brien had long gone for the day, and Jennifer knew she should be leaving soon as well, but there was something going on that surely had an explanation. On one of the Dorchester certificates she calculated the difference between five percent and six percent and combed the debit columns for that amount but did not find it. She had no expectations of finding it in the scribbled sheets of the credit columns, but find it she did. The exact amount to the penny. He mind raced over what she had done and all the possibilities for error on her part.

But she did not see an error. She saw a debit amount for the six percent interest charged the customer against the balance of the certificates' worth. And in the credit column she found the difference between five percent and six percent added back as if there had been an error in the calculation. A cold chill ran over Jennifer's back. She would need to check the cash balances for that day and determine if someone with the mysterious initials had returned the cash or debited another account balance for that amount on that day. But there was no time for it today, she thought, bile rising in her throat at the thought of dinner with her mother and Jeffrey.

* * *

"You are late for dinner," Jane said as Jennifer entered the dining room. "Punctuality is required in this household as you well know."

"I'm terribly sorry. I was delayed," Jennifer said. She'd been sitting at her dressing table, fully clothed, hair styled and jewelry attached, thinking about how much she was dreading even the sight of Jeffrey Rothchild. The butler seated her, and she was forced to look up at him observing her with cold, dead eyes from across the table. She swallowed and looked away.

"How were your travels, Jennifer?" he asked.

"Very nice," she answered with a shaky voice. "You may have heard my sister Jolene and her daughter traveled home with me."

"She is dining with her husband's family this evening," William said.

"They are no one you need to know or worry about, Jeffrey," Jane said with a smile and a nod. "Jolene will not be in Boston long enough to cast a shadow on our Jennifer."

"The Randolphs have sent us an invitation to their dinner dance. It is two weeks from Friday," Jeffrey said.

"I was just telling Jennifer that she and I must get to the dressmaker. She must have something exquisite to wear," Jane said.

"Please send me the bill for this dress, although I highly doubt anything could be as exquisite as Jennifer herself," Jeffrey said.

"No," Jennifer said while her mother tittered. "That will not be necessary."

Jennifer chewed the beef Bourguignon their French chef had prepared as if it were the cover of a bank ledger book and barely tasted her wine, satisfying her thirst with water. She concentrated intently on keeping her hands from shaking as she lifted her glass or dabbed her mouth with the linen napkin. It would not do to allow Jeffery to see how much she was rattled by his presence. She must adopt Jolene's advice to appear calm and unafraid even if she were terrified.

After dessert, her mother rose, and smiled at Jeffrey. "I am feeling a bit tired tonight. Please excuse me if I do not visit with you in the parlor. Perhaps Jennifer can entertain you in the music room. There will be no one to disturb you there. William? Will you escort me to my rooms?"

Jennifer was glad then that she had not eaten much, as her stomach rolled over as they walked down the long hallway to the music room. Jeffrey opened the door and she preceded him inside. She hurried to the bench side of the piano.

"Did you not receive the letter that I sent you before I left for Washington?" she asked.

"Yes. I did receive it," he said, and looked around the room before settling on her face. "That O'Brien woman? She was speaking to one of my clerks today. Someone told me she works with you in the parlor lobby. What on earth was she doing interviewing my clerk?"

"I don't know," Jennifer said and watched as Jeffery took slow, measured steps across the room, stopping near the open end of the grand piano.

He tilted his head at her. "Come now, Jennifer. I have read your letter. Come sit down in front of the fire. You look like a terrified child. We will discuss this letter you have sent."

He was right. She *was* acting like a terrified child, and giving him the advantage. She came around the piano and seated herself near the fireplace in a chair. Jeffrey raised his brows and sat on the sofa nearby. "There is nothing to discuss about the letter. I no longer desire your company," she said.

"Why on earth not?" he asked. "Our marriage is sanctioned by your parents and unites two old families, and there certainly is a spark between us. We will manage fine in *all* aspects of our marriage."

A shiver trailed down Jennifer's back. The idea of kissing Jeffrey, making love to him was repugnant. What she had found attractive at their first meeting had been quickly diminished, replaced by fear and loathing. She was certain if she married this man, he would rule her in all aspects of her life, and force her to his will in the marriage bed. There would be nothing pleasant about it, except, perhaps, for him.

"There will be no marriage, Jeffrey," she said more firmly. "You cannot force me."

"Really?" he said, and laughed softly. "Do you really think I would play this game without having all the cards in my hand? I will fire O'Brien Monday morning. I will not have her snooping about in places she does not belong."

"No!" Jennifer cried. "No! She has done nothing to you. She works for me!"

"No one works for you. You are a hostess, I have come to understand. But clearly she does not know her boundaries. I'm a vice president, Jennifer. I can fire whomever I want."

"Please, do not do this."

"Please, you ask? You'd best save your requests for favors. And if you continue on with your attempts to end our engagement, you will begin to hear rumors about your mother," he said. "That she is mad."

She stood abruptly. "You would not! How dare you!"

"I would not? I certainly *would* dare," he said with a laugh and rose from his place. "So innocent you are, my sweet one. It makes me want to steal a kiss from my intended."

Jennifer backed up until she could feel the fire's warmth on her back. She glanced left and right for a way to escape but he was touching her before she could move, holding her upper arms in a tight grip.

"Quit fidgeting, Jennifer. I am going to kiss you. You'd best get used to it, as I will require your services every morning before I leave for the bank."

She braced herself as he kissed her hard, breaking the skin on the inside of her lower lip as he bit her, holding her cheeks tightly with one hand. She pushed at him with her free hand, but it was useless. He was strong and she was at his mercy. Tears pooled in her eyes. She grabbed wildly for the mantel, hoping to reach a candlestick or a book. He pushed her away from him for a brief moment.

"If you hit me with something it will go doubly worse for you, I promise," he said, and slapped her backside and hip hard with his swinging open hand, stinging her flesh and leaving her senseless for a moment.

Jennifer's cry was swallowed by him as he kissed her again, shoving his tongue in her mouth. She went limp.

"I'm sorry to interrupt. I didn't know anyone was in here."

"Get out!" Jeffrey shouted.

"Your father is looking for you, Miss Crawford. May I take you to him?"

"Yes, oh yes," Jennifer said and wiggled out of Jeffrey's hold. "Do excuse me. My father is looking for me."

Zeb pulled her arm through his and led her down the hall, patting her hand as he went. She stared straight ahead and consciously slowed her breathing. She was out of Jeffrey's clutches. Out of the room. But what would she do to guard her friends and family from him? She realized then that Zeb was seating her in the parlor by the fire and handing her a glass and a hanky. She looked up at him. He was an intense man, she noticed then, staring at her in such a way that she could feel the power and concentration emanating from him. She was not frightened but rather reassured by the way his energies surrounded her.

"Thank you," she whispered, and stared into his eyes.

Zeb took the handkerchief from her hand and dabbed her mouth. She sat motionless until he pulled it away and she saw the bloodstain. Her hand went to her lips.

He knelt in front of her. "You must tell me what I can do for you."

"Nothing." She shook her head.

"I don't believe you."

"You must believe me," she pleaded. "There is nothing anyone can do for me."

He searched her eyes. "Rothchild is hurting you or threatening you."

"No, no," she said and looked away from him. "It was just a misunderstanding."

"Have you spoken to your father about his behavior?"

She shook her head. "My father needn't be burdened. He is troubled enough as is."

"Your father would not want to see you hurt."

"And sometimes we are not the only ones who could be hurt," she replied and pulled her hands from his.

"Just because you give me these cryptic answers does not mean I don't understand. He's hitting you and threatening those you care about. I've dealt with his type before. He will only back down when met with opposing force. Let me have a word with him. I'll keep you safe. I swear."

There was little doubt in her mind that Zebidiah Moran would keep her safe and be her champion. But there was nothing he could do to help O'Brien. And most of all there was nothing he could do to help her family if Jeffrey spread rumors that Mother was mad. Jolene even believed it was true, making it less of a rumor and more of a secret. What would that do to her mother's fragile health and her father's equilibrium? What could he do, after all, in the banking world and among Boston's highest social class to keep her family from becoming a laughingstock? Banks had shuttered their doors over information such as this.

"Please do not speak of this again to me, and if you would be so kind, do not repeat your concerns to anyone else. I will manage this in my own way," Jennifer said and looked at him. "Will you promise me?"

"You've given me no choice, have you?"

"Not if you respect me and my wishes."

Zeb laid his palms on her cheeks. "I respect you, and I care for you. I think you harbor similar feelings for me but are frightened. I sincerely hope I do not scare you."

She opened her eyes and watched as his face came closer and closer, until his forehead touched hers. She breathed in the smell of him, of soap and bay rum, and man. How easy it would be to run away, to live with Jolene, and to see if something would come from being in company with Zeb Moran. But life was not that easy, not her life anyway. She had her parents to think of, of Willow Tree and all of its staff, and the bank, too, her legacy, her family's legacy. She could not waltz away as if none of it mattered, even with this glimpse of a life with this man. She could not.

Jennifer stood abruptly and hurried to the parlor door. "Thank you for escorting me from the music room. I must retire now. You know the way to your rooms?"

"Yes," he said.

* * *

Jennifer arrived early at the bank on Monday morning. She'd stayed in her rooms most of the previous days and thought about what she would do about Jeffrey Rothchild and had made some decisions. She was going to speak to him about the threats he'd made and stop silently acquiescing to his demands and moods. Certainly she could make him see reason, and perhaps she misunderstood what he said about Mother. She must have a positive outlook; far too much hinged on her managing the situation in the best interests of the bank, her family, and her own sanity. She took a deep breath and knocked on his office door.

"Good morning, Jeffrey," she said and forced herself to smile at him.

He rose from behind his desk and buttoned his jacket. "What a pleasant surprise. Please come in."

Jennifer steadied her eyes on his. "I'd like to talk about our last encounter."

"Really?" he said, and indicated a chair. "I'm not sure there is much to discuss, but I certainly wouldn't want anyone to think I didn't indulge my future wife."

"I'm here to ask you not to fire O'Brien or spread rumors about my mother."

Jeffrey tilted his head and smiled at her. "And?"

"And, well . . . I'm asking you to not fire O'Brien. She is here only to serve as a chaperone for me in the parlor lobby. I have no idea why she asked your clerks anything, but I will have a direct conversation with her and instruct her to never do such a thing again. As for the comments you made about Mother, I don't imagine that it would be good for the bank's reputation for that sort of thing to be said publically. Our fortunes, yours and mine, are tied directly to the success of this bank."

"Touché. However, you must remember, I came to this bank with considerable wealth of my own. I will never be destitute."

She met his gaze. "True. But there is no doubt of your plans. You wish to marry me to secure the bank as your own. Father will retire at some point and his daughter's husband will move into the chairman's suite. You would hardly risk that, would you?"

"How clever you are, Jennifer! It will be useful to have a wife with insight and intuition." he leaned forward, glaring at her. "Just as long as you speak only to me on such matters. I will not have a wife who makes herself look ingenious to anyone other than her husband. It is unnatural, and such a wife would be punished for it."

Jennifer backed up in her chair at his tone, and his seething contempt for her. "I understand," she whispered.

"Good," he said after staring at her for some long minutes. "And since you have been so cooperative, I will not fire your friend O'Brien."

"Thank you," she said, and hurried from his office. They had not discussed his threats about her mother, but she could not stand to be in his presence one more moment. She had thanked him for not firing O'Brien. How foolish and scared she'd been! As if she was required to thank him for every small relief he gave her. But perhaps she was.

Why didn't she just walk away from Jeffrey? Refuse to see him? And yet she knew the answer to that question. She knew that it was not in her nature to make a scene or openly defy someone. She'd been the peacemaker all of her adult life, and perhaps when she was a child as well, placating her mother, consoling her father, calming servants who had been in her mother's purview. She did not want shouting and hysteria and managed the middle ground between her parents and others. How pitiful she was!

Jennifer arrived at the bank the following morning with renewed enthusiasm for the Dorchester portfolio. After she had spoken with Jeffrey the previous day, she and O'Brien had been able to narrow down the initials to four bank employees. She told O'Brien to make no more inquiries for fear that Jeffrey would hear of them. They had agreed that the initials in question looked as though someone was deliberately making the letters illegible, and it worried Jennifer excessively to think that someone at the bank was stealing.

Jennifer knew she must speak to her father about it soon and wasn't sure how to begin. He considered the bank employees, from the kitchen staff to the clerks to the men in high positions to be his family, in a manner of speaking, and made sure employees with an ill relative or a tragedy like a house fire were well taken care of. He would be devastated to find out someone had been stealing from him. She and O'Brien had not broached the word "theft" in their conversations but she believed they had the same suspicions. They would discuss it today.

But they did not. O'Brien did not come to work, which was unusual for her, nor had she sent her younger brother to Willow Tree with a message as she had done on other occasions. Jennifer was peeved at O'Brien but spent her day busy entertaining clients with only a few scant hours to examine the books further. By midafternoon she was exhausted and sent for her carriage. She had her driver take her to the house adjoining Willow Tree stables, where O'Brien and her father and younger brother lived. She'd made herself angry over O'Brien's absence but chided herself for being unduly upset with the woman, who had become a friend. Jennifer knocked on the O'Brien door. The stable master opened it.

"What are you doing here?" he said gruffly.

"I . . . I stopped to see your daughter. She did not come to the bank today and I wondered if she was unwell or if there is something else the matter," Jennifer stuttered, and took notice of his unshaven face, bloodshot eyes, and disheveled clothing as she followed him inside.

"Yes, there's something the matter, girl," Thomas O'Brien said. "There's plenty the matter! But we need none of your help."

"Mr. O'Brien! What is it?" she asked.

But the tall, muscular man just stood there, hands on his hips, clearly furious. Then his shoulders dropped and he sat abruptly in the kitchen chair behind him. He rubbed his hand over his face, and tears tumbled down his ruddy cheeks.

"What has happened?" Jennifer said. "Where is she?"

"The doctor is with her now," he said and gazed at the staircase. He looked at Jennifer. "I fell asleep reading in my chair by the fire last evening and woke when I heard what sounded like a kitten crying at the door. It was no animal. It was my Kathleen."

Jennifer sat down beside him, watching him wipe the tears from his face. She leaned forward. "Please, Mr. O'Brien. Tell me."

The older man nodded. "'Twas her. 'Twas my Kathleen. Broken and bloody on the stoop. I carried her inside and sent for the doctor. He came and worked on her 'til dawn and he came back now to check on her. She cries out though as if whatever happened is happening again and again." He stopped crying and looked directly at Jennifer. "She went to the Robinson Theatre with someone she met at the bank earlier in the evening. Said he was a real gent and that he was even a friend of your intended. I never thought twice about letting her go, I'm sorry to say. The theatre is only down the street and she said there were other young people going. I never thought . . ."

Jennifer watched O'Brien drop his head in his hands and sob. She turned to the sound of a man's voice.

"Thomas," the doctor said as he came into the kitchen. "She's going to live, I believe. I've bound her ribs. There are three broken but none have punctured her lungs. The bone around her eye is shattered. What I did last night is probably the best we can do without surgery. She's going to lose some teeth, but not the front ones. And we've got to watch that cut on her chest. I've stitched it shut but I'm worried about infection. She's alive, Thomas. She's still alive."

Jennifer stood, as if in a dream. She turned away from the doctor now patting Thomas O'Brien on the back. She walked to the steps and up them, trancelike, not conscious, but not so far away that some terrible truths were not able to begin to take hold in her mind and make her queasy. She walked down the hallway to where O'Brien's brother sat on the floor near a door, his head on his knees. She touched the doorknob and looked at the blood on the door and its frame before opening it.

She took a deep, gulping breath at the sight of her friend and tears streamed down her face. She smoothed O'Brien's hair. "O'Brien," she whispered. "Who did this to you?"

O'Brien's uninjured eye flittered open and she panicked, struggling against Jennifer's hands and making terrified guttural noises in her throat. She finally connected with Jennifer's eyes and looked past her, wildly writhing as if to see someone else in the room.

Jennifer shook her head. "There is no one with me. Your brother is guarding the doorway, and your father and the doctor are guarding the door to this house. It is just you and me. Calm yourself. *Shhh.*"

O'Brien shook her head.

"You must be calm," Jennifer soothed, and opened the drawer on the nightstand beside the bed, finding a pencil stub and a scrap of paper. She put the pencil in O'Brien's hand. "Tell me who did this to you. I am terrified at what I am thinking. Please tell me."

O'Brien clutched the pencil and waved it at her.

"Paper. Yes. Here is paper, O'Brien. I will hold it for you. Tell me," Jennifer begged.

After some struggle, O'Brien scratched two words. Jennifer turned the paper around to read them but it did not say a name. It said merely, "be terrified."

She looked at O'Brien and their eyes met. There was no mistaking the message even with no words between them. O'Brien grabbed her hands then, and Jennifer held the paper for her again. She knelt on the floor to watch as O'Brien wrote.

"B. F. J.," Jennifer said. "What does that mean? What does it stand for?"

But O'Brien was running out of energy. She scrawled "initi" before her hand fell away to the bed.

Jennifer stood and looked down at her friend. "Initials. Those are the initials that we were unable to decipher. Those are the initials of the person who attacked you. It is connected."

O'Brien nodded once, and Jennifer kissed her forehead. "Do not worry about anything. I will see that your father has help and that you have the best care and that there are guards at your door if you feel it necessary. Do not worry. Rest and I will be back often."

* * *

Zeb watched the door to the parlor as he waited for dinner to be announced, and socialized with Jolene and her father. Jane Crawford was on a settee with Jeffrey Rothchild, whom he'd been formally introduced to on his arrival. The man had quickly turned back to Jennifer's mother, as if Zeb were as insignificant as a worm under his polished boot. Jane and Rothchild had their heads close together now and Jane was patting his hand, and looking at him from under her lashes.

There was not an ounce of doubt in Zeb's mind as to who was tormenting Jennifer. He recalled the look on her face when he'd interrupted her and Rothchild's embrace in the music room. She had looked up at him when he said her father was asking for her and the look on her face was combination of terror and helplessness that had made him swallow back his anger and hatred for the man and concentrate on escorting her somewhere she could compose herself. She could not bring herself to look him in the eye otherwise.

"I had best check on Jennifer," Jolene said. "I don't know what could have kept her so long."

Zeb looked up just then and saw Jennifer, standing outside the door, one hand on the doorframe as if to steady herself and the other fisted tightly at her side. She was pale and took a deep breath before coming into the room. She avoided her mother and Rothchild and made straight for her father's side.

"It is time for dinner, Bellings has just told me," Jennifer said in a breathy voice. "Please escort me to the dining room, Father."

Zeb winged his elbow for Jolene to take as they passed Jeffrey, now assisting Jane from the settee. "Your sister is white as a ghost."

"She is," Jolene replied. "I stopped in her room earlier and she was shaking and near tears. She told me that her companion at work was severely beaten last night. O'Brien is her name, and she is the daughter of the man who manages the Willow Tree stables. She is a well-educated young woman and has known our family since she came here with her father years ago."

"Beaten?"

"Yes. The doctor that attended her feels she will live, but she has broken bones and is cut deeply on her chest. Jennifer has told Cook to send three meals a day to O'Brien and her family and to have a maid attend them once a day to clean and wash laundry and help with changing dressings and that sort of thing. Mrs. O'Brien died during the same flu epidemic that claimed my son, William. Few families were untouched."

"I'm sorry to hear about Miss O'Brien," he said. He watched Jennifer and her father ahead of them walking down the hall to the dining room, she hanging on to her father's arm, even leaning her head against his shoulder as they walked.

"Here, Jennifer," her mother said once she was seated. "Sit between Jeffrey and I. We have much to talk about with the Randolph dinner dance coming soon."

Jennifer stood stone-still, not looking at anyone as her father moved to his seat at the other end of the table. Jolene swept past her.

"But Mother," Jolene said as she circled past her mother's chair and seated herself between her and Rothchild. "We've had so little time to chat, and I haven't had the opportunity to get to know Mr. Rothchild."

Zeb held a chair for Jennifer beside her father and then seated himself across from her.

"I am anxious to hear of your work in service to the Crawford Bank, Mr. Rothchild. Please tell me every detail," Jolene said, snapping open her linen napkin and forestalling a comment from her mother.

"How are you today, Miss Crawford?" Zeb asked.

She looked up and took a sideways glance at Rothchild. "I'm sorry. I didn't hear what you said, Mr. Moran."

"I was wondering how your day was, Miss Crawford. It was a pleasant temperature out of doors, and I wondered if you'd been able to enjoy it," he replied.

"I did not notice, the temperature, that is," she said softly.

"It has been comfortable as of late, even for a late-night stroll," Rothchild said. "Although going out alone without the company of family is never prudent for a young lady."

Jennifer looked up sharply, startled by Rothchild's words. He appeared pleased he'd been able to do so, staring at her still and smiling.

"I heard today that your friend O'Brien was set upon and severely beaten last evening," Rothchild said, looking at her over his wineglass as he took a sip. He sat the glass down and picked up his knife and fork, poised to cut the braised beef on his plate, but stopped and looked at Jennifer again. "Not your concern, my dear, as it is already being said that she was not a well-bred woman. Perhaps she taunted one of her lovers too far."

Jennifer's fork clattered to her plate. She was staring at Rothchild with a dawning recognition for what he implied—that her friend was somehow to blame for her beating.

"Mr. Rothchild," Jolene said. "The O'Briens have been with us for decades, and Miss O'Brien was educated at one of the better schools in the city. I will not have you cast aspersions upon her name; I'm sure you are well ready to apologize to me and to my sister Jennifer. Perhaps you do not understand the nature of the relationship between the O'Briens and the Crawfords."

Rothchild laid his silverware down neatly on either side of his plate. Zeb could see Jolene's face, stern with one raised brow, and he recognized the haughty tone of her voice. It served him well as Zeb was inclined to pick Rothchild up by the throat and send him flying through one of the long windows. The father, though, was finally paying attention.

"Apologize to whom?" Jane Crawford said. "The girl is beneath our notice. Why shouldn't Jeffrey believe what is being said about her? She is a servant and always acted as if she were more than she was, more than just the daughter of a man who mucks out our stalls. The lower classes are noticeably without morals. You will have nothing more to do with her, Jennifer."

Tears were running down Jennifer's face when she stood and threw her napkin down on the table. "That is enough, Mother. More than enough. I cannot abide your hatefulness," she said, and hurried to the door.

The dining room was silent for a moment until Zeb heard the scrape of Rothchild's chair and watched him hurry to the door of the room, but not before stopping to bend over Jane's hand. "I will go and speak to your daughter, Mrs. Crawford. She certainly misinterpreted what I said and was disrespectful to you. I can't imagine what has caused this overemotional response during polite dinner conversation."

Rothchild turned from Jane to find Zeb standing in the doorway. It was clear that he thought Zeb would step out of the way, with one intimidating glance. "Perhaps Miss Crawford would like some quiet time," Zeb said.

"This is no concern of yours," Rothchild said and shot his cuffs. "She is my concern and my fiancée."

"Really? Is she your fiancée?" Zeb asked quietly, meeting Rothchild's glare with one of his own.

"Mr. Rothchild? Please come back to the table," Jolene said. "Your meal is becoming cold. Would you like me to have it warmed?"

Rothchild turned to look at Jolene, glanced back at Zeb, and returned to his seat. He turned to Jane.

"I have a surprise for you Mrs. Crawford," he said. "I have obtained tickets to Sir Benedict Fitzhugh's talk and was hoping you would accompany me as we both have an interest in science."

Jane leaned forward in her seat. "Fitzhugh? You have attained tickets for Fitzhugh? How wonderful! After our discussion last week I am very interested to hear the man speak!"

"Fitzhugh?" William Crawford said as he sliced another piece of meat. "Don't remember hearing about him. What particular discipline does he discuss?"

"It is all very exciting—" Jane began but was cut off by Rothchild.

"He studies the stars. Really remarkable man, educated at Oxford. Your wife has shown an interest in such matters, and I thought I'd return your frequent hospitality to me by escorting her to hear this lecture," Rothchild said, and smiled cordially at William.

William waved his fork. "By all means. I'm in your debt for seeing to Mrs. Crawford's entertainment."

Chapter Nine

JENNIFER STOOD STARING AT HERSELF in the long mirror in the ladies' retiring room in the Randolph mansion. She had wondered all week why she was as weak-willed as she was. Why what she convinced herself she would do, she didn't do when the time for a decision arrived. She did not wish to go anywhere with Jeffrey or even speak to him, but here she was arriving at the Randolphs' dinner party with him. Jolene had insisted on riding with her in Jeffrey's carriage, much to Mother's dismay. Jeffrey was openly hostile to Jolene, who responded as if he had not been rude to her in the least. Mother was furious, of course, with everyone but Jeffrey.

Jennifer straightened her gown a final time and opened the door.

"I thought perhaps you had become ill, Jennifer," Jeffrey said as she opened the door, and he shrugged away from the wall.

"Perhaps I am ill," she said, suddenly furiously angry at herself for not going directly to the police with her suspicions about Jeffrey and O'Brien's attackers. She started down the hall without stopping to wait for him. "Perhaps I am sick of you."

He grabbed her arm and swung her around to face him. "What did you say?"

"I said I am sick of you. What will you do, Jeffrey? Will you hit me again? Perhaps blacken my eye in a crowded ballroom?" Jennifer whispered.

Other guests turned the corner at the end of the hall and Jeffrey attempted to pull her close as if they were lovers in an embrace. Jennifer stepped out of his reach.

"I am going to find my father and sister," she said.

Jeffrey followed her until they joined her parents and Jolene. He quickly turned to her mother. "Mrs. Crawford, won't you please allow me to introduce you to some young men and women of good families that I am acquainted with? The young ladies especially are very excited to meet you."

"How lovely! Of course I will meet your friends," Jane said, and patted her elaborate hairstyle. "Young people do gravitate to me, you know."

Father smiled and nodded while Jolene pulled a face. "How ridiculous she sounds when she speaks to him," she whispered to Jennifer as she looked around the room. "Ah. There is someone I was hoping to meet again."

Jennifer looked through the throng of faces. "Who would that be, Jolene?"

"Lenora Gladfoote," Jolene said. "I am a happy and contented woman, but who wouldn't take the opportunity to share her husband's recent senatorial election and business fortunes with an old nemesis. And how fortuitous that I am wearing the large and rather gaudy diamond ring that Maximillian insisted I have when I announced I was expecting. I shall wave it in full view."

Jennifer watched as Jolene raised her hand and called to her old friend. "Why Lenora! How marvelous to see you!" Jolene was quickly gathered into a tight crowd of beautiful, well-coifed women and the men at their elbows.

Jennifer smiled and accepted the glass of wine that her father brought her. The crowd parted, and she had a clear view of her mother surrounded by people her and Jeffrey's age. Did none of them think it strange that he was introducing her mother rather than *her* to his friends, although she herself had no interest in meeting any of them? But then she noticed several of the young women catching each other's eyes as if privy to a private joke. Jeffrey was standing beside Mother, but slightly behind her, too, and Jennifer was certain her mother could not see the faces he was making, the raised eyebrows and wry smiles that he was sharing with the other young men.

"You do not know your science very well, young lady," Jane Crawford said loudly enough that heads turned.

Jennifer made her way to the crowd but other young people were gathering around after hearing the tittering and giggles, and she could not get close. But she could hear.

"Sir Benedict is a brilliant man, I'll have you know. I was fortunate enough to hear him speak recently on the subject. His credentials are impeccable! I was even able to speak to him briefly, was I not, Mr. Rothchild?" Jane said and looked over her shoulder.

An appropriately serious Jeffrey nodded. "Yes, Mrs. Crawford. You were indeed fortunate to meet such a . . . brilliant person and have his undivided attention."

"He was very attentive," Jane said, and winked at one of the young women. "He referred to me as 'the queen of Boston society.' What fine manners he has for an academic. He'll be speaking in New York within the month at one of their leading universities."

"What a ninnyhammer," whispered a young woman to her friend, both standing just in front of Jennifer.

"Who is this Fitzhugh fellow who is so enamored of her?" the friend whispered back, and giggled at her own joke.

Jennifer wondered the same but did not have to wait long for the answer as a young, dark-haired man, full of himself, smiling at her mother and winking at Jeffrey, asked a question. "What of his 'moon creatures,' then? Has he seen any recently?"

"Well," her mother replied, "he has not had any recent sightings using his telescope at the Vienna Observatory; however, others here in the States have invited him to use their observation equipment and confirm their findings."

"Really?" the dark-haired man said. "How remarkable! So others are seeing the creatures as well?"

"Yes!" Jane replied enthusiastically. "And some have even spoken to them."

The crowd erupted in jeers and laughter. Jennifer pushed her way through the throng, pardoning and shoving her way until she was beside her mother.

"Come along, Mother," she said and took hold of her elbow. "Father is wondering where you are."

"I'm speaking to Jeffrey's friends. As you should be doing as his fiancée," she replied, and shrugged off Jennifer's hand.

"Rothchild's fiancée?" the dark-haired man asked. "Why has there been no announcement? No engagement soiree for the happy couple?"

"I am not . . ." Jennifer began until she looked at her mother's furious, red face. She looked up at Jeffrey, at his smug smile, and realized that much of this was by design, to humiliate her mother and to publically announce their engagement, making it much more difficult to refute in the future. But any denial now might prompt her mother to make more of an embarrassing scene than had already been accomplished.

"Perhaps one of Fitzhugh's 'moon creatures' can conduct the ceremony, eh, Mrs. Crawford?"

"How ridiculous," her mother replied. "They are not here. They are on the moon."

"Maybe Fitzhugh will fly his space carriage up there and bring one down!" someone shouted from the back of the crowd.

"Perhaps he will!" she said in retort. "He confided to me that he is building one!"

Jennifer took her mother's arm again. "Mr. and Mrs. Randolph are looking for you, Mother. Let us go and find them."

But Jane stood immobile suddenly, her face white, and her hand trembling in Jennifer's. She clutched her stomach, closed her eyes, and doubled over.

Jennifer held her mother close to her side and looked for a way to exit the gathered crowd. One young woman asked Jennifer if there was anything she could do to help, and she sent her for her father or Jolene.

"Clear the way," Jeffrey said then and bent down to Jane's face. "I will find you a place to rest. Lean on me now."

"Oh, yes, please," Jane said to him and allowed him to hold her by the waist and guide her out of the crowd through a path that had magically opened.

Jennifer followed and saw her father hurrying to them and Jolene not far behind. Jennifer turned to the door and found a servant to ask that the family carriage be brought to the door immediately.

* * *

Zeb wandered through Willow Tree, passing servants, all of whom asked if they could help him or get him anything, or show him to the library. He declined their assistance and instead continued walking the wide hallways until he passed a doorway that servants were coming from and going into. He opened the door and found a stairwell leading to a labyrinth of rooms, including a massive kitchen.

Cooks, maids, and housemen all were at work, doing their assigned duties. A short, round woman approached him.

"Are you looking for Mr. Bellings or Mrs. Gutentide, sir?" she asked.

He smiled and shook his head. "I don't know who I'm looking for. I wanted to speak to someone who knows the O'Briens and may be willing to introduce me to them."

Several people stopped what they were doing and looked at him. Others gathered around him. An older man looked at him from the top of his head to his shoes. He took a sliver of wood out from between his teeth. "Who's asking?" he said.

"My name is Zebidiah Moran. I'm here at the request of Senator Maximillian Shelby, to see to the safety of his wife, Mrs. Jolene Shelby, and her sister, Miss Jennifer Crawford."

"How do we know you're who you say you are?" the man asked.

"He's telling the truth," a brawny young man said as he leaned against a doorframe. "I took Miss Jennifer's and Eliza's trunks on the train to Senator Shelby's home last month. Delivered them as I was told to do a day before they arrived. Saw this gent. The houseman said he was aide-de-camp to the senator."

"Why on earth would the trunks not travel with them on the day they went, Luther?" someone asked.

Luther shrugged. "Don't think the mistress wanted anyone to know she was going."

"That's enough with the gossip," an older, distinguished-looking woman said as she made her way down the hallway. The crowd dispersed as she came, other than the man with the sliver of wood, once again between his teeth, and Luther, now standing straight, arms crossed in front of him.

"I didn't say nothing out of turn," he said.

"May I help you, sir? I'm Mrs. Gutentide, the housekeeper here at Willow Tree."

"I imagine you heard my introduction, ma'am. I am interested in meeting the O'Briens."

"You do understand that Miss O'Brien has been injured? Most brutally."

"I do, ma'am. I am hoping to speak to Mr. O'Brien about it."

Mrs. Gutentide looked at Luther. "Have you carried over the evening meal for them yet?"

"Clarice is packing it now."

She turned back to Zeb. "Walk to the stable house with Luther when he delivers their meal. He can ask Mr. O'Brien if he is willing to speak to you."

"Thank you, ma'am."

Zeb followed Luther through a formal garden and a series of gates to a large horse barn and a gabled house nearby. The grounds were well-manicured and the buildings recently painted. He would have dearly loved to be talking to Mr. O'Brien about the horses he bred and tended, but that was not his mission this evening. He waited at the end of a stone walkway while Luther carried a wooden box into the house. Moments later, Luther emerged from the house, turned and pointed to Zeb, and spoke to a man in the doorway. The man walked slowly down the walk. He stopped when he was six feet away.

"What are you doing here?"

"I'd like to speak to you and your daughter, Mr. O'Brien. My name is Zebidiah Moran."

The man rubbed his chin, looked away out over the yard, and back at Zeb. "What are you wanting to talk about?"

"I'd like to find Miss O'Brien's attackers."

"What is my daughter to you? How do you know her?"

"I don't know her, only that she was an innocent, and badly beaten. I am here at Willow Tree to keep Senator Shelby's wife and her sister safe."

"Then why are you here and not at the Randolphs' party with Miss Jennifer and Miss Jolene?"

Zeb smiled. "There are security men at the Randolph estate, of course, and I have hired private individuals to guard them on their way there and back to Willow Tree. I deemed the occasion a low enough risk that I could rely on others, and make inquiries elsewhere about your daughter's attackers."

"And why is it of interest to you?"

"I believe there is a connection between Jennifer Crawford and your daughter and their mutual safety."

O'Brien took a deep breath. "You may as well come inside. But let me be clear. I will find who did this to my Kathleen and I will kill them. Neither you nor any of your policemen or Pinkerton agents will stop me."

Zeb followed O'Brien inside, not doubting for a moment that the man was telling the truth. A burly, red-headed man sat in the corner of the room, a rifle across his legs. The man stood, looked Zeb up and down, and went to the door. "I'll keep watch outside, Thomas."

Zeb sat where O'Brien pointed, at a long table near a roaring fire. O'Brien dropped two glasses on the table and a corked bottle. He poured them both a jigger.

Zeb sipped the whiskey and took a good look at Thomas O'Brien. The man was unshaven, unkempt, and wearing clothes that had not been recently laundered or pressed. "How is Miss O'Brien?"

"As good as can be expected for a girl who's been beaten and tormented," her father said with a sniff. "The doctor thinks her eye is healing well. One of the stab wounds became infected but it cleared up quick, and he doesn't think there'll be much of a scar."

"I am glad to hear that she is doing better."

Zeb heard footsteps on the stairs, and O'Brien stood up quickly. A young boy appeared.

"What is the matter, Sean?" O'Brien asked. "Does your sister need something?"

"She wants to know who is here," the boy replied.

"Go back up and tell her there is nothing to worry about. McGuire is outside with his shotgun and I am in the kitchen. She is safe."

"Who is in the kitchen, Father?" they heard from above stairs.

O'Brien hurried to the steps. "You are safe, Kathleen. Go back to your room."

"Who is it?"

"It is the man sent to guard Miss Jolene. He is no threat to us."

"Mr. Moran?" she called down the stairs.

"Yes, Miss O'Brien?" Zeb said as he stood.

"Why are you here?" she asked.

Zeb glanced at Thomas. "I was hoping to ask you some questions regarding your attack, Miss O'Brien. I am glad to hear your recovery has begun."

"There is no need, Kathleen," O'Brien said, even as Zeb heard soft footfalls descending. "Mr. Moran was just leaving."

Zeb watched as the young woman took two hesitant steps into the room. Her left eye was still swollen shut, and the entire side of her face was brown and blue. There was a yellow bruise on her chin, and he could see where the split on her lip was scabbed over.

"What questions?" she asked him.

"Anything you can remember about the man who hurt you."

Kathleen O'Brien walked to the massive stove and her father and brother followed her as if she were going to crumble or faint at any moment. He watched her shoulders rise and fall when she stopped at the glass-doored cabinet holding dishes. "Does anyone care for some tea?" she asked.

"Is this wise, colleen?" her father asked softly.

"I cannot be prisoner in my rooms for the rest of my life, Father. And I fear the longer I wait the more difficult it will be to ever leave."

Thomas wiped the back of his hand across his eyes. "Then it's tea we'll have. Sit down now. I'll see to it."

Zeb watched as she slowly turned to the table. His first instinct was to hurry to her, pull out her chair, and help her be seated. But he was fairly certain she would have crumbled as her father and brother suspected she would if a man she didn't know got close to her. Young Sean was at his sister's side then, pulling out her seat and unhooking her shawl where it had caught on the chair. He patted her shoulder awkwardly.

"I'll stand by the door if you'd like."

Kathleen smiled and leaned her head against his arm. "I'd rather you sit here beside me and have some tea. McGuire is outside standing watch. Who would get past him?"

Thomas filled two flowered cups and set them in front of his daughter and son. "Are you warm enough, Kathleen? I can add some wood to the fire or fetch a blanket for your legs."

"I'm fine, Father. You will have Mr. Moran thinking I'm more of an invalid than I already am."

"I think you are far from an invalid, Miss O'Brien. I think you are a survivor, and I think your brother and father just want you to be safe."

She stared at her hands for some time. "I have already told the police everything I can remember."

"Do you remember much of the attack?" he asked.

Her head came up sharply. "Yes. Yes, I do. Every night when I close my eyes, it's as if it is happening all over again."

"What are you able to tell me about it?"

"It was dark. He was tall and smelled like the fish market," she said as her hand came to her neck. "I tried to scream, I think. Maybe I did. And then it was black."

"You were alone?" he asked.

"Yes. I had gone to the Robinson theatre with some friends and was walking home. I should have never walked down that street. I knew it wasn't safe."

"Don't blame yourself," her father said as he came to stand behind her.

She looked up at him and patted his hand as he held her shoulder. "I do blame myself. I was wrong."

"You were at the theatre with friends and they let you walk home alone? I am surprised." Zeb looked up at Thomas O'Brien.

"I thought the same thing, Moran. What kind of men were they? Nothing like what I would have done when I was a young man. These young people today are lazy."

"I didn't want to put them out. They were going the other direction," she said. "I've told you all of this, anyway. I don't blame them."

Zeb stared at her until she looked at him. He was going to take the risk of being bodily thrown out of the O'Brien home, but his concerns weren't with this well-guarded young woman, but rather with Jennifer Crawford, whose risk he believed was greater than originally imagined.

"Begging your pardon, Miss O'Brien, but I think you're lying."

"Get out!" Thomas screamed. "Get out!"

The door to the house flew open and the man with the shotgun charged in. "What is it, Thomas?"

Zeb sat purposefully still and stared into Kathleen's eyes. Tears were rolling down her face. "You are protecting someone by withholding the truth," he said amidst more shouting and threats. "You are protecting Jennifer Crawford, and perhaps your family as well."

"Stop! Stop this shouting and screaming," she said finally. The room silenced immediately. "Thank you, McGuire. I am fine but would be more comfortable if you were on the outside watching for intruders. Sean, it is nearly time to feed the horses. Perhaps you can help the stall boy."

Thomas sat down. "What haven't you told me?"

She covered her mouth with a shaking hand. "He whispered in my ear, you know. Said that Sean would have an accident and that there were ways to discredit you. That you would lose your job and we'd be living on the streets."

"What did he say about Jennifer Crawford?" Zeb asked.

She looked up. "That she'd be used foully by several men and she'd be glad that Rothchild would still have her. That she would learn to like a good smacking before servicing her husband."

"Why didn't you tell me any of this?" her father asked. "It must be someone who knows you through your work or knows Miss Jennifer to know so much about us. We can make inquiries . . ."

"No!" Kathleen cried as she stood abruptly, knocking her chair over behind her and pounding her fist on the table. "Don't you see? They will get to her! You will watch out for me and for Sean, but she has no one! You must not tell anyone what I have said. There is more to this than . . ."

"Than what? What is this about, Miss O'Brien?"

She shook her head. "Leave it alone. You must not interfere."

"I can't. I *won't* leave it alone. I'm going to keep her safe. Do you know who attacked you?" Zeb asked.

She gathered her shawl around her and walked to the steps. "I am tired and want to rest. Good day to you."

Thomas watched her retreating footsteps. "Contrary like her mother. Thinking she needs to keep me safe. As if I wouldn't work in the sewers to feed my family."

"She's a very brave young woman. She feels she needs to protect Miss Crawford. Please pass on to her that I will be seeing to Miss Crawford's safety personally," Zeb said as he let himself out. He had much to think about. But he was unable to sort out his thoughts sufficiently to begin to plan. All he could hear repeating through his head was "she would learn to like a good smacking." It made him want to puke in the trimmed hedges as he made his way back to the main house of Willow Tree.

Chapter Ten

JENNIFER WAVED TO HER FRIEND Ruth Edgewood Mullens across the dining room of the Parker House Hotel dining room. She'd left Eliza in the lobby with enough coins to find a suitable establishment for her luncheon and instructions to return in an hour. Her father's insistence over the years that she have a maid accompany her in public seemed silly for a modern young woman near the turn of the century, but Jennifer did not resist the company any longer. After O'Brien's beating she was hesitant to move about the city alone even during daylight hours as she had been doing for years.

"How glad I was to receive your note, Ruth!" she said as she kissed her friend's cheek.

Ruth squeezed her hands. "It is so good to see you. Our sporadic luncheons and brief moments spent together at a tea or a dinner just don't do."

"I agree." After they had perused the menu and gave their orders to the waiter, Jennifer said, "So tell me about Harry, Mr. Mullens, that is. How is married life?"

Ruth smiled. "It is wonderful. I am very happy and contented. Of course, Harry is so gentle and kind and considerate of me, I could hardly be otherwise!"

"I am so very glad for you," Jennifer said, and listened as her friend described the excitement of her recent wedding trip and Harry's business success.

Jennifer wasn't sure when, but she had given up on having the kind of closeness and adoration Ruth felt for Harry for any partner she might have. It was increasingly mentioned how fortunate she was to be engaged to Jeffrey Rothchild. It was as if because it had been said at the Randolph party it was now real and true. She didn't know what to say when an acquaintance said something about it. If she denied it, she would embarrass the speaker and herself, and she didn't really know how to explain it away. She'd told a friend of her father's that she and Jeffrey were not engaged, and the fellow commiserated with her over having to break off something as formal as a marriage engagement in such a public way. She hadn't the heart or the stomach to tell him there'd never been an engagement to begin with.

"I've been asked by several people if you and Mr. Rothchild were engaged, and I told them absolutely not as you would never become engaged to be married and fail to mention it to me," Ruth said and smiled. "Unless of course there is some happy news you would like to share now?"

Jennifer shook her head. "No. I am not engaged. I will never marry Mr. Rothchild."

"Oh. That is rather final. I am sorry to hear that things did not turn out as you anticipated. I remember speaking to you this past summer and you seemed quite taken with him. I was so hoping you'd found your special someone as I have."

"He is not special. Nor is he anything like I'd thought he would be. It is strange, though, that he *seemed* to be a perfect fit for me, and knew so many of the same people, and just, well, looked like he would be the perfect husband. How silly of me to think that what a person looks like would be indicative of their character."

"It sounds as though your opinion is quite set, but just a few days ago someone mentioned your relationship with Mr. Rothchild to me. Yet it appears that there never was much of a relationship to begin with. Gossip about your family doesn't ever seem to end," Ruth replied.

"About my family? Have you heard something other than Jeffrey and me?"

Ruth's face reddened. "That was poorly said. I didn't mean to imply . . ."

"I think you have heard something else. Please tell me."

"It is nothing, I am sure," Ruth said and shrugged.

"Then why won't you tell me?"

"It's just that my mother heard that your mother was unwell at the Randolph dinner. Mother was unable to attend as my sister Lydia had just presented her husband with their first child and Mother had not yet traveled back from Ohio. But she was at one of her committee meetings last week and someone there, well, several ladies there, remarked that your mother became ill at the dinner party. I'm hoping she is feeling better."

"Ruth. We have known each other since we were girls at Ramsey. There is something you are not telling me. I can see it in your face."

Ruth looked down at her plate and put down her silverware. She looked up at Jennifer. "It was said that your mother was acting strangely. That is all. I'm sure it was just because she was feeling unwell."

"Tell me."

"I have no wish to hurt your feelings, nor do I feel right about carrying tales that are surely spoken out of malice. You must believe me."

"I don't believe for one moment that you intend to hurt my feelings, but it really is best that I know what is being said."

Ruth looked away and back at Jennifer with such a pitying face that it was all she could do not to shake her oldest and dearest friend by the shoulders until she sputtered out all the worst things that she imagined people were saying about her mother.

"It is being said she is a devotee of Benedict Fitzhugh and that she defended him and believes all of his tales. It is being said that she attended one of his speeches here in the city with Jeffrey Rothchild and that Mr. Rothchild said that he had no idea who this Fitzhugh fellow was and that he was just doing a favor for his fiancée by taking her mother to what he thought was going to be an academic lecture. It is being said that she believes in moon creatures and that perhaps she is not mentally well."

Jennifer took a deep breath and thought about all the falsehoods contained in those few sentences and how they were close enough to the truth to be quite believable. "Has there been any mention of my father?"

Ruth slowly patted her mouth with her napkin. "Only that he found his wife's behavior unremarkable."

"And by not denouncing it, he is condoning it."

Jennifer ate her food and listened to her friend attempt to lighten the mood with stories about her brothers and sisters, whom Jennifer had been acquainted with as long as she knew Ruth. She waited with Eliza under the massive gold-colored canopy of the Parker House Hotel for their family carriage to be brought in front. Eliza was talking about a dress she'd seen in a window as she'd walked back to the hotel. Jennifer nodded in the appropriate places as her maid elaborated on her find, but she replayed in her mind all that Ruth had said. All that was being said about her, about Jeffrey and Mother, and her father. She was going to visit O'Brien that evening and share with her all she'd discovered lately about the Dorchester portfolio and ask her directly who had attacked her. At each of her visits with O'Brien, they'd shared knowing looks when the subject came up but nothing was ever spoken aloud, nothing was for certain. Jennifer needed certainty.

* * *

"I'm going to visit Miss O'Brien, Mrs. Gutentide. Is there anything I can deliver for you?" Jennifer said later that day in the kitchens of Willow Tree.

"Yes, Miss Crawford. There are these cleaned clothes to be returned. But they may be too heavy for you. I'll get Luther to carry them for you."

"I'll carry them for Miss Crawford," Zeb Moran said.

Jennifer turned. "I did not hear you behind me, Mr. Moran. I'll be fine. There are only a few things, and Mrs. Gutentide has them folded neatly in a bag."

"All the same," he said, and reached past her and picked up the cloth sack.

"Thank you, Mrs. Gutentide," she said, and went up the stone steps that opened to the walkway between the stables and the main house. She stopped, turned, and held out her hand. "I can carry the bag."

"I'm happy to carry it for you. Will you mind company on your walk? I was hoping to talk to you."

"I do not need nor do I want your help. You are employed by my brother-in-law, not my father!"

Jennifer felt tears at the back of her eyes and her hands were tight fists at her side. She'd been nursing an ache in her head since early that morning, mostly she imagined because she slept little as of late and inevitably woke with stiff, clenched shoulders, in a cold sweat, regardless of how thin and light her sleeping gown. Zeb Moran was staring at her, watching her take deep, gulping breaths.

"It is as though I opened my mouth and my sister Jolene spoke, was it not? I did not mean to sound shrill or rude. Please just give me the laundry," she said.

"May I speak boldly?" he asked.

"Would there be much I could do to stop you?"

"Very little. Can we sit at the bench there?"

She led the way and pulled her wool cape tight around her as she seated herself. "What is it? I have promised my friend O'Brien I would visit this afternoon."

"I have recently visited with Miss O'Brien. I would be happy to go with you and see her again."

Jennifer looked up. "I'm sure you have not. She has been very particular about whom she sees and Mr. O'Brien guards her closely."

He sat down beside her and looked her in the eye. "But I have. I have sat with her father, met her brother, Sean, and had a rather enlightening conversation with Miss O'Brien herself."

Jennifer looked away. "I hope you did not frighten her. Aside from her injuries, she is still not . . . herself. What could possibly be enlightening about a conversation between total strangers?"

"Perhaps I went as a gentleman, concerned for a young woman who is recovering from an attack."

"But you did not, did you?"

"I asked her what happened the night she was beaten."

"I do not understand why any of those details would interest you, but she has spoken to the police and to the Pinkerton agents about that night. It is hardly kind to make her relive it."

"I asked, and she told me that her attacker was tall and smelled like a fish market."

"Then she has told you the same as she has told everyone else."

"I told her she was a liar."

"You what?" Jennifer cried as she stood. "How dare you? How dare you badger a young woman who has been brutalized?"

"Please sit down."

"I will not! I will not sit, and I won't allow you to speak so cruelly to my friend!"

"Calm yourself and let me talk to you. Easy does it," Zeb said as he stood and wrapped his hands lightly around her upper arms.

"She has done nothing to you. Why torment her?"

"She has done nothing to me, but she has done something *for* me. She has confirmed my deepest fears. She told me and her father that you and her brother and father are in danger. Serious danger. She pounded on the table when her father said he'd share this information with the police. She feels there is no one to guard you and that you will make an easy target. She has been protecting you all along."

Jennifer stilled. "She must be mistaken."

"No, she's not. She's not mistaken. She told me what the man said to her, but there is something she is not telling me. I can't protect you if I don't know all the details."

"What did she tell you?"

"She told me that her attacker said that her brother, Sean, would have an accident and that her father would be discredited," he replied.

"She is terrified that her brother will be hurt. I think that is the thing that most haunts her. Although the idea of something happening to the horses in her father's care is very upsetting to her as well. She has grown up riding and caring for these animals and is very attached to them."

"I believe Miss O'Brien and her family and the horses are reasonably well-guarded. I understand Mr. O'Brien has friends who take shifts guarding the house and the stables."

"Yes, they do," Jennifer said.

"What I don't understand," he said, "is why the guards were not hired by your father?"

"There is no need to understand as this is none of your business."

"What is truly puzzling, though, is why you are angry with me and do not hesitate in the least in telling me so but you continue in a relationship with a man who treats you badly. Is hitting you and threatening you, I think."

Jennifer felt the blood drain from her face, but did not consciously feel her arm lifting and her hand landing, open palm, on Zebidiah Moran's face. Nor did she anticipate her fingers stinging with the blow or the look in his eyes. In an instant, she was frightened, and horrified at what she had done. She turned and ran toward the staff entrance, praying the kitchens would be empty. She did not make it far, though. He was suddenly in front of her.

"Stop running, Jennifer. Talk to me," he said.

She could not explain, or begin to understand, why she was doing exactly as he described. Why was she rebuffing the care of a man, and "rebuffing" was too small a word to describe what she had just done, to keep peace with a man who was threatening her very existence and the security of her family? "Why are you asking me these questions?"

"Perhaps because you won't ask them of yourself."

Tears filled her eyes. "I am a coward. I know I am. But I'm unable to change. I'm afraid and silly and cannot seem to . . . t-to," Jennifer stumbled. "Why do you continue to be kind to me?"

"I was raised a Southern gentleman. My mother would have tanned my hide had she heard me being anything less than that," he said and smiled at her. "I may earn another slap, but you have not been yourself since coming here. Although you were quiet when you first arrived, you were different when you were staying with your sister. You were happy and relaxed. You seem to me to be everything *but* happy and relaxed here in your own home."

She dabbed her eyes. "You cannot understand the implications of the situation I am in. You know nothing of Boston society or our family business. I must solve these issues in my own way, on my own."

"I do not understand Boston society, or even your or your family's place in it, but I do understand men like Jeffrey Rothchild. His kind of intimidation happens in the cheapest saloon, the most luxurious boardroom, and in the kitchens of everyday families. You are not unique nor do you need to manage this yourself. Please don't call yourself a coward, either. You are not a coward. You are facing an enemy alone; however, that is not necessary. Allow me to help."

She stared into his eyes. "I am shaken to my core. What I've always thought I could discern about another person has been proven to be completely and utterly wrong. The stakes, the consequences of my poor judgment, threaten the Crawford family, threaten those that depend on us, threaten the fortunes and the legacy my family has built. Where Jolene expected a lifestyle of wealth as our due, and Julia naively assumed that everyone lived as we did, I knew differently. I know that the kind of wealth and prestige our family enjoys is the product of incredibly hard work, perfect timing, and considerable luck, otherwise, every other family in America would be wealthy and enjoy a home such as Willow Tree with all of its amenities. That existence hangs in the balance. I will not allow this generation to fritter it away."

"I am unable to help you with Boston society or your family's business, but I do think you need to hear the truth. Ask your friend Miss O'Brien what was whispered in her ear concerning you when she was attacked. It may be true that you must navigate Boston society alone, but you must be safe while you do so or all of your work and worry is for naught. I will see to that."

"So you are proposing to keep me safe while I tend to what is necessary?"

"Yes. I will escort your sister back to Washington as planned later this week and return to keep watch. You will become very tired of seeing my face but you will be free to do whatever is needed to get your family ship righted."

"Mr. Rothchild will not care for it. Neither will my mother."

"That is not my concern."

"What will Max say? You are his employee. He may not allow you to leave for any extended amount of time."

Zeb took her hands loosely in his, touching his thumbs to her palms. "I am employed by the senator, not owned by him. I will suggest he appoint a new chief of staff."

"You would give up working for my brother-in-law? A prestigious, challenging position? I listened to you and Max speaking about your bills and procedures and how future generations will benefit from the laws you are writing and hoping to pass. You would give that up? But why?"

He stared at her then, looking into her eyes, past her fears, past her hurts and torments, to her. To the place deep inside her where her heart and soul beat. Where all the worldly adornments and entrapments of wealth and obligation were stripped away and did not influence her feelings or hopes. Where the essence of *her* recognized *his.* She was not breathing, nor did she feel the cool breeze at her back.

"I don't have a choice, you see," he said in a whisper. "The only thing I know is that I must keep you safe, that that is more important than any future outcomes or past consequences. You can relax, you can breathe easy. No one will ever strike you or threaten violence against you on my watch. I promise you that and would die fulfilling it."

Tears streamed down her face although she was not sad or fearful. "You would let me win my battles at the expense of your dreams?"

"There is no cost too high for your safety and happiness."

Jennifer touched his cheek, still pink with her handprint. "I am so sorry. I am unable to even touch my mount with a crop and yet I lashed out in anger at someone who has done nothing but be kind to me. Have I become the tormentor?"

Zeb covered her hand with his. "No. But you are frustrated and frightened. I believe you and Miss O'Brien have uncovered something unsavory at the bank, and it is difficult to know how to proceed when you are scared for your life. It is no longer necessary to be afraid."

"It is no longer necessary to be afraid," she repeated. She believed him. Zeb Moran, even in his expertly tailored jacket, snug trousers, and flat satin waistcoat, exuded a dangerous physicality. She'd watched him rope horses and carry feed and lift calves in his dungarees and flannel shirts while in Texas. She'd wiped the sweat from his chest and lanky arms, strung through with muscle, when she nursed him through the influenza. He was manly and lovely, she'd admitted to herself at the time, and his body was so different from her own. But here now, in his formal clothes, with his brown-gold hair touching his collar in a curl, his chest just inches from her breasts, she'd never felt safer, or more attracted to a man. For him to touch her, caress her, run his fingers the length of her, and she him.

Jennifer leaned forward and touched her lips to his, for just a moment. She could smell his soap and feel the bristle of his beard against her chin. He was breathing quickly and staring at her mouth. He touched her cheek and pushed his fingers through the loose strands of her hair, holding her head lightly in place, as he touched his tongue to her lips. Jennifer groaned with the heat of it, wishing every inch of her body was touching his.

"I want to kiss you, Jenny," he whispered.

"Is that not what we are doing?"

"I want to hold you. I want to cover your mouth with mine. I want your breasts and your hips tight against me"—he pulled away to look into her eyes—"but I don't want to scare you."

"I am not frightened of you. Please," she said, although unsure of what she was asking.

Zeb wrapped an arm around her waist, pulling her to him until her body was flush against his. With a last survey of her face, he focused on her mouth and claimed it, pushing his tongue through her parted lips. She clutched his shoulders where her hands lay, relishing the friction and heat on her breasts where they pressed against the stiff fabric of his jacket. He angled his mouth over hers, and ran his hand up her side, his fingers just grazing the side of her breast.

He pulled his lips away and laid his forehead on hers. "I've been dreaming of kissing you since the day I woke up from fever. But I couldn't imagine such a fine and bright woman as yourself ever dreaming of a scoundrel like me."

Chapter Eleven

JENNIFER HAD SPENT THE LAST hour pacing her rooms, deciding what would be the next wise thing to do. She was feeling lighthearted, gay even, thinking that she was no longer worried about Jeffrey. She would be able to say what she wanted to him with no fear of reprisal. She wondered why she hesitated to be forthright with her mother and father as well, and she could not think of one reason that was justifiable. She was an adult and well educated. She managed all the consequences of her mother's manipulations with staff and family anyway. Why appease someone who would not be mollified? She was going to be kind, but straightforward, lifting the veil from her father's eyes and challenging her mother rather than acquiescing to her constant demands and wishes. Jolene's advice finally made sense.

Her newfound confidence ebbed when she spoke to O'Brien.

"What did he say?" she asked her friend as they sat beside each other on O'Brien's bed. "You must tell me."

O'Brien stood and wandered to her window. "I was hoping to shield you from all this with my silence. Hoping to convince you that the Dorchester portfolio balanced. How I was going to do that, however, is a stretch of the imagination as I can barely step over the threshold of my home without crying and shaking, let alone go back to the bank, to my work that I love. As much as I hate my attacker for the violence he perpetrated on me, I hate myself more for being terrified."

"I know of what you speak," Jennifer acknowledged, after taking a deep breath. "Mr. Rothchild has hit me on two separate occasions. My ribs were broken, I believe, the first time. I am so sorry to have dragged you into this."

"I'm so sorry for you. I've found that violence like this affects the mind as much as wounds on the body."

O'Brien sat down beside her. The two women held hands as if facing their tormentors, staring ahead out the side window of the house to where the winter landscape was giving way to spots of green. “He said you’d be used foully by several men, raped and ruined, and that you’d be happy that Rothchild would still have you, if you weren’t with child. He said that you would learn to like a good smacking before servicing your husband, as you would be doing whenever and wherever Rothchild wanted.”

Jennifer shivered and fought the bile rising in her throat. Tears filled her eyes. “Sometimes I believe the terror of my imagination is more horrible than what could actually happen. But how ridiculous! When I think about the pain, the humiliation, and embarrassment that followed after he hit me, I am certain my imagination cannot match.”

“I can smell my attacker’s breath, I swear, when I wake up in the middle of the night,” O’Brien said. “I can feel his spittle hit my ear and cheek as he whispered all the foul things that would happen to my father, and to Sean and to you.”

Jennifer rose. “Mr. Moran is going to see to my safety, personally. I will no longer be in a position to be tormented by Jeffrey Rothchild at home or at the bank. When you are ready, I am certain he would guard you, too, if you chose to come as well.”

O’Brien wrapped her arms around herself and shook her head. “No. I can’t. Please do not ask me to.”

“Do not worry one second. Stay here and get well and let your father and brother care for you. You are barely out of your sickbed!”

“I cannot do it.”

"Then you must not."

* * *

"Father, may I speak to you?" Jennifer asked as she stepped through the door to his study.

"Certainly, my dear. Have a seat. Shall I ring for coffee?"

"If you wish, Father. I have some important things to discuss with you."

"Important things, my dear?"

Jennifer watched a maid roll in the coffee cart and proceeded to pour for her father. But she did not sit down when she finished. There was too much at stake to be casual. "I believe O'Brien was attacked because of what she and I have discovered at the bank."

"At the bank? How could that have anything to do with what happened to Miss O'Brien? She should have never been on that street. It is unsafe, and she is the proof."

"No Father. It was not random. She was a target, and her family was threatened."

"You must have the wrong of this. Perhaps she is hysterical."

"She is terrified. Not hysterical."

"It is a horrible lesson learned for a young woman. Her father is surely tormented by it."

Jennifer stepped closer to the desk and waited until her father placed his cup that he had been contemplating in some seriousness in its saucer and looked up at her. "O'Brien did nothing wrong. There was no lesson as a consequence of bad behavior, but there was a message. She was attacked because we have found something unscrupulous in the Dorchester portfolio and have been making inquiries about our concerns."

"Unscrupulous? How absurd! There has been a mathematical error made. That is all."

She shook her head. "You are wrong, Father. I believe someone is pocketing money and hiding the difference in the percentages the bank charges in interest."

"That cannot be. We could see it if the debits and credits did not balance."

"It is hidden in the credit column as if the pilfered funds were redeposited."

"But then we would see it in the cash balance."

"I suppose it depends on the accountant who is doing the cash balance for that month."

William Crawford rose from behind his desk. "Are you implying that one of the vice presidents of the bank is falsifying records?"

"Yes, I am," she said. "I cannot yet prove it—"

"Of course you can't!" he shouted. "Because it is not true!"

"I cannot yet prove it, but I believe Jeffrey Rothchild is embezzling money."

"Jeffrey Rothchild?" her father said in disbelief. "*You* asked me to hire him after you had just met him last spring! Yet you went to your sister's last month to escape him and an impending engagement, but at the Randolph dinner you were his fiancée. And now you are accusing him of theft? You must say nothing about this to anyone! We could have a run! Rumors such as this have brought banks to their ends before, and if word was out, Jeffrey would never be hired in Boston again!"

"You are concerned about *Jeffrey*?"

"Of course I am! He is a vice president of the Crawford Bank! Any aspersions cast upon him will reflect on the bank. People will say that you have argued with your fiancé and now are spreading rumors about him. We do not need anyone to know about this or speculate on the bank's liquidity or trustworthiness. You must obey me on this."

"It would be better for these *errors* to be exposed during a bank audit? We would never survive the aftermath. Creditors would be lined up at our door if the Comptroller of Currency for Federal Banks were to find an inconsistency."

Crawford dropped into his seat and stared away at the fire burning brightly in the fireplace. He sat silently for some long minutes. "I will look into this personally," he said, and looked up at Jennifer. "But I will not have a good man slandered over delicate female sensibilities. I have dealt with that all of my life."

"Female sensibilities?" Jennifer whispered. She should tell her father now, right this very second, she thought, about Jeffrey's violent nature. But she did not. How could she reveal that she'd allowed it? That perhaps she was deserving of it? And what would she do? Open her blouse and lift her chemise and show him the faded bruises?

She had just recently concluded that perhaps she'd sought out the man who would be able to humiliate her much like her mother had done to her all of her life. That she was accustomed to that treatment and comfortable with it. Wasn't that what was said about children and their parents, after all? Her father had concluded she was the manipulative one and cruel like his wife, and she'd always viewed herself as a victim of Jane's moods, or insanity as Jolene insisted, and now Jeffrey's. And beyond it all, she was still embarrassed and now more than ever knowing that her revelation provoked her father to be compassionate to another of his gender who was at the mercy of the females in his sphere. But had she not just promised herself to convince her father otherwise?

"You will find I am right about the Dorchester portfolio. I never once said I was Jeffrey's fiancée at the Randolph party, but it was said by *someone*. I didn't deny it because Mother was ill and she had already made herself look a fool. I didn't want to fan any fires."

"A fool?" he said and rose, wandering to the window and presenting Jennifer with his back. "She seemed quite popular with the young people."

"Popular? Her preoccupation with Fitzhugh made her a laughingstock."

He turned. "Do not speak of your mother this way. It is not dignified."

"Oh, Father," she said, and shook her head slowly. "There is talk about Mother . . . about her peculiarities. Her behavior reflects on the bank as well. We are in a precarious situation."

He turned to the coffee cart, refilled his cup and looked up at her with a smile, as if the previous conversation had not happened. "More coffee, my dear?"

"No, thank you," she said. "I must check in with Mrs. Gutentide on this week's menu."

* * *

"You consider this serious enough that you would quit working for Maximillian?" Jolene asked Zeb.

"Yes. Your sister has not told me the details, but I feel her life is in danger," he said. "I will escort you back to Washington and then return immediately to Boston."

"If it is that dangerous, you must stay with Jennifer. We will make some other arrangements for my travel."

"No. I will not break my word to Max. I will see you home and travel back the following day. I have contracted with a young man working at Willow Tree. Luther is his name, and he has been in your family's employ since he was very young and is a friend to your sister's maid. Luther is to guard Jennifer as best as he is able. I told him if he is dismissed or threatened, he will come work for me. Miss Crawford has no outside engagements for the time I am away so I am hoping all will be well until I return."

Jolene sat stiffly in the brightly flowered settee in the study of her brother-in-law, Calvin Billings, her hands folded in her lap. "It is Mr. Rothchild, is it not? What has he done to her?"

"It is not my secret to tell. But I will not allow anything to happen to her. I will guard her with my life as I have already told her," he said.

Calvin touched Jolene's shoulder. "If for any reason Mr. Moran cannot return by Sunday evening, Eugenia and I will arrive at Willow Tree, collect Jennifer, and be her escort at the Boston Hospital Soiree. I will not let her out of my sight, and Mr. Moran has already arranged for additional protection at the hotel."

"Have you spoken to my father about your concerns?" she asked.

Zeb shook his head. "That is for your sister to do, and I'm not sure he would believe me anyway."

"Maximillian is not going to like this," she said. "He considers Jennifer to be in our family sphere. He is going to want to take the next train to Boston and have a word with Mr. Rothchild."

"Max has state matters that must keep him in Washington. I have already spoken to your sister. She has agreed to allow me to guard her while she solves . . . other issues."

"What other issues?" Jolene asked. "You must tell me."

Zeb shook his head. "It is not my place to say, but she has not told me either. You should talk to your sister before you leave for Washington."

"I will. I'll be dining at Willow Tree tonight."

He sat down beside Jolene. "Please do not allow yourself to be alone with Mr. Rothchild. I believe the point of his aggressiveness is your sister, but he has already proven to be the type of man who would use terror to get his way. I cannot sufficiently guard both of you, and I will be focusing on Miss Crawford's safety as I think she is the one most at risk."

"So I shall pretend to be helpless and not stray far from my father's arm?" Jolene said and raised her brows. "And how ridiculous you sound referring to Jennifer as Miss Crawford. You are in love with her. There is no need to stand on ceremony with me or with Calvin, as he is my family, and therefore Jennifer's as well."

"I never said, I would never presume to . . . Miss Crawford and I have no understanding other than that I will guard her as she goes about her business and the bank's business."

She rose and straightened her dress. "I have no doubt you would slay a battalion of men for the safety of my sister. You are brave other than in matters of the heart. I will speak to Jennifer this evening and unearth her secrets if she is willing to share them."

Zeb watched her sweep out of the room, her yellow silk dress swirling, leaving a rose scent in her wake. Calvin Billings was staring at him. "She is the most exasperating woman I have ever had the misfortune of knowing. How Max lives with her is a mystery," Zeb said.

Calvin laughed. "Max is hopelessly in love. He dotes on her and she him. Jolene can be sharp-tongued but she is not stupid. In fact, she is very perceptive."

Zeb stood outside of Jennifer's room that evening waiting to escort her to dinner. It would doubtless be interesting or contentious, as Jeffrey Rothchild would be joining them that night at Mrs. Crawford's request. He had watched the man himself enter the front doors a few minutes ago from his vantage point on the second floor balcony across from Jennifer's suite, and drop his hat and coat into Bellings's arms with no acknowledgment that the butler existed other than to serve him.

On his way from Calvin Billings's home, Zeb had stopped the Willow Tree carriage driver six blocks away and walked the final distance to clear his head and think about what Jolene had said. *Love? This was love?* This ache he felt when he saw Jennifer? This nearly uncontrollable urge to shoot Jeffrey Rothchild between the eyes even if it meant prison or worse? But more than all of it, more than anything, he longed to see her smile. There was nothing in his world or memory to compare to what he felt when she looked at him and smiled. When he evoked her image in his mind it was of the night of the ball in Washington when she was talking about her work at the bank. Her face was radiant, and she was lovely, as she spoke with enthusiasm and passion for the work she did. The door across the hallway opened.

"Mr. Moran. You are waiting for me here?"

"Yes," he said, and pushed himself away from the ornate bannister. "I want to make sure that I escort you into the dining room myself."

"Yes, of course," she said. She looked at his arm as he held it out for her, hesitating as if taking it spelled some greater commitment than walking beside him down the staircase.

They entered the dining room, and Jeffrey turned to her from where he stood beside William Crawford. His smile faded when he saw her arm looped through Zeb's. Rothchild walked directly to them.

"You may release my fiancée," he said.

Zeb looked down at Jennifer. "Miss Crawford, which seat would you like to take? Perhaps here beside your sister and father?"

Jennifer nodded, careful to not meet Rothchild's eyes.

"There is a seat beside me and we have much to discuss, Jennifer. Come," Rothchild demanded and winged his arm for her to take.

"She's already chosen her seat," Zeb said, steering her past Rothchild's arm and holding her chair out until she was seated and her skirts tucked beneath her. He moved a mere foot away from her and stared at Rothchild.

"You had best find the kitchens, boy," Rothchild said. "I won't have you being so familiar with my fiancée."

"Jennifer!" Jane Crawford said from her seat at the head of the table. "Mr. Rothchild wants you to sit beside him. How rude you are being!"

Jennifer turned her head to her mother. "I prefer to sit here."

"How formal we are being," Jolene said, and walked to the seat beside Jennifer. Zeb pulled out her chair. "There is an open seat to Mother's left, Mr. Rothchild. We didn't assign seating this evening."

Rothchild rounded the table and seated himself with a flourish, nearly knocking over the young man holding his chair. Zeb left Jennifer's side then, and walked to his seat beside Rothchild.

"The Boston Hospital Soiree is Sunday evening next," Rothchild said to Jennifer. "I will be escorting you, and we shall set the date of our engagement party. My secretary will see to the invitations. Send your list to him."

Jennifer was staring at Rothchild, white-faced, except for the red flush climbing up her neck. "I don't believe—"

"Jennifer," Rothchild interrupted with indignation. "We needn't argue over trivialities in front of your family. As I've mentioned before, there are always consequences when a couple disagrees publically."

Jennifer flinched noticeably, and Jolene was staring at Rothchild with a venomous look that even a man as predisposed as Rothchild was to being exclusively concerned with himself could barely miss.

"Miss Crawford will be escorted to the Boston Hospital Soiree by Mr. Calvin Billings and his wife, Mrs. Shelby's sister and brother-in-law. The arrangements have already been made," Zeb said and smiled at Rothchild.

"Well, you must undo them, Jennifer," Jane said with a huff. "Those people are nothing. We mustn't be seen as advancing them. You will go with Mr. Rothchild. It is settled."

Zeb leaned forward in his seat and met the mother's eyes. He smiled. "No, Mrs. Crawford. It has been arranged and will not be changed. Miss Crawford will be attending with the Billingses."

"That is enough," Rothchild said and slammed his silverware down on the table. "You will leave this house at once. Of all the impertinence!"

The room was silent other than the hiss of the taper candles. Zeb picked up his spoon and began eating his soup. He swallowed, tapped his mouth with his napkin, and looked at Rothchild. "No. I am not leaving. The soup is delicious, by the way."

"It is delicious," Jolene said and turned to Jennifer. "Isn't oyster stew your favorite?"

Jennifer looked from one face to the next. "It is my favorite. Even when I was a young girl. Wasn't it, Father?"

Jane was sputtering her indignation, and Rothchild turned in his seat. "I am telling you that you need to leave this house at once. This is a fine old family with a reputation to keep. We don't need an upstart with no pretense to civility at this dinner table. Leave at once."

Zeb shook his head. "No. I'm staying. Try the soup, Mr. Rothchild. It is delicious."

Rothchild looked at William. "This man is disrupting our dinner and upsetting the ladies, Mr. Crawford. I shall call Bellings to have him removed."

"I am not leaving, Mr. Crawford. Your cook is to be complimented. Dinner is delicious," Zeb stated.

William looked up then, gazing from face to face. It would be awkward to stay at the table if this man attempted to have him forcefully removed but Zeb did not think it would come to that.

"Lamb for the main course, I believe. Cook's lamb is a triumph," Crawford said as he concentrated on his soup.

Rothchild was seething, visibly angry, and stayed that way for the course of the meal. After dessert was served, he rose and walked to Jennifer's seat. "Come along, dear. We have much to discuss."

"There is no one in the music room, Jeffrey. You may entertain Jennifer there," Jane said.

Jolene stood, and wrapped her arm around Jeffrey's. "I will be happy to play for our entertainment."

Zeb was already at Jennifer's seat. "Music would be very nice," he said.

Both couples walked through the door. Rothchild shook off Jolene's arm. "I am going to have a private discussion with my fiancée. Get out of here, the both of you," he ordered, and made a grab for Jennifer's arm.

Zeb moved Jennifer behind his back. He shook his head. "No. You will never be alone again with Miss Crawford. Is that understood?"

"You have no idea what you are saying or whom you are saying it to," Rothchild growled. "You are nothing."

Zeb shrugged. "I am the something that is not going to allow you to be alone with Jennifer Crawford."

"Jane! Jane!"

They all turned to the dining room doors as they flung open and servants hurried out. Jennifer, Jolene, and Zeb went inside to see Jane Crawford slumped in her husband's arms as he shouted for the doctor to be fetched. Zeb caught Luther by the arm.

"Make sure Mr. Rothchild is escorted out of Willow Tree."

William Crawford carried his wife up the grand staircase, his daughters and several servants fluttering behind him. Dr. Roderdeck was called, and Mildred prepared Mrs. Crawford's bed. Zeb followed behind, one eye on Jennifer and one on Luther handing Jeffrey Rothchild his coat and hat. He watched as the door to Jane's suite closed and reopened moments later when William came out, slowly closing the door behind him and staring at him as he stood across the hallway.

"My wife is ill," Crawford said, glancing back to the door he had just closed. "The doctor says she needs an operation, but Jane says she will have none of it. I'm at loss as to what to do." He looked then at Zeb, narrowing his eyes, in a way that made Zeb think that he had just noticed who he'd been speaking to. "Who has employed you to interfere with Rothchild?"

"I have hired myself."

"Don't be glib, young man. I understand you were hired by Jolene's husband to guard his wife. What puts Jennifer in your purview?"

"Rothchild is dangerous. His family fortunes are not as solid as you may think, and he is desperate to marry your daughter and solidify his position at your bank."

"And what of your finances? The secretary to a wealthy man, yes, but you may be just as much a fortune hunter as you say Rothchild is."

"I am no fortune hunter. My wealth is more than ample, and is diversified in many investments including stocks, land, and bonds," Zeb said. "Feel free to examine my bank accounts."

"Then what are your interests in my daughter?"

Zeb stared at Crawford. "She is vulnerable, and I want to take away her fears and worries. I want her to smile."

* * *

"Dear Lord, I am exhausted," Jennifer said as she sank into the flowered chintz sofa in her rooms.

"It is nearly midnight," Jolene said from the stool she sat on close to the fire. "I thought Dr. Roderdeck was never going to leave. Even aside from the fact that mother called him a Polish spy."

Jennifer rolled her neck from side to side, slipped off her shoes, and pulled her feet underneath her. "She fired one of the cleaning girls last week and told Mrs. Gutentide that the girl had devil eyes and was casting a spell on her while she slept."

"She is paranoid, that is for certain. Mildred is even beginning to be frightened of her. She told me tonight that mother accused her of poisoning her food."

"Mother is in so much pain," Jennifer said. "I wish she would take the laudanum the doctor prescribed until her surgery."

"I can hardly believe she agreed to it."

"What choice does she have? Dr. Roderdeck was clear that she has little chance of surviving if she does not have the surgery and even then . . ." Jennifer sniffed. "I do not want her to die. Even knowing how cruel she can be."

"Of course you don't. None of us do," Jolene said and stood, stretching her back and then taking a seat beside her. "Zebidiah came to see me this afternoon."

Jennifer turned to her sister. "You'll be planning your return trip. I'm sure that Max is looking forward to seeing you."

"Zebidiah did come by to tell me that we are leaving Saturday morning for Washington, and that he will be making an immediate return to see to your safety," Jolene said and stared at Jennifer. "How remarkable, I said to him at the time, as her family knows nothing of a threat to her safety."

Jennifer looked at her hands. "Perhaps Mr. Moran is exaggerating."

"I don't believe he is."

"What did he tell you?"

"Nothing, or at least very little. He feels you are in danger but will not tell me why. He has hired one of the servants here, a friend of your maid Eliza's, and I would guess he is rather physically intimidating, to guard you while he is taking me back to Washington. He said you need to be safe while you address other issues. He did not betray you. What are the other issues?"

"Mr. Moran is a gentleman, after all," Jennifer mused. "He would not speak out of turn."

"Tell me," Jolene insisted. "Tell me every sordid detail if there are any. Mother is ill, father is beside himself, and we must rely on each other."

"I am so embarrassed! And foolish! I hardly know where to begin," Jennifer said, with a shake of her head.

"How did you meet Mr. Rothchild?"

"Last spring at one of the first garden parties. I'm not even sure which one anymore. I thought he was the most handsome man I'd ever seen. He made it clear from the beginning that he was interested in me, and there were very many lovely young ladies in attendance," Jennifer whispered. "He fussed and fawned over Mother and Father. What a fool I was."

"We are all fools at some time. Go on."

"I met him on several occasions over the summer, and it was clear to me at the time that he angled to be seated next to me, or dance the first dance or the last with me. I was flattered. I thought he was in love with me."

Jolene shrugged. "Of course, you would think that. Why wouldn't you?"

"I have not had many serious admirers, as Mother remarked often, and for once, she and I were in agreement that Mr. Rothchild was handsome and charming. It is so exhausting to be at odds with Mother constantly. She thought Mr. Rothchild was everything that I could wish for in a husband, and I believed her, or I *wanted* to believe her. But he did present himself as a prosperous man from a good family, who'd been educated well, at least in the beginning."

"You are assuming far too much blame for whatever predicament you are in," Jolene said. "Mr. Rothchild is a handsome man, and he wore the right clothes and used the correct fork and spoke in a way you were accustomed to. We are all drawn to what is familiar, to what seems normal, but those things are mostly superficial. One never knows another person until they have spent some time with them and seen them under duress. Once you did spend some time with him, I believe you discovered something unpleasant, and meant to distance yourself from him."

Jennifer looked at her sister. "Yes. That is exactly what happened. Yes."

"I know it is what happened because you have always been the good and dutiful daughter, and even having a mother such as we do has never influenced your natural kindness. You have been witness to multiple family crises and have managed to stay neutral and calm. I admire you."

Tears filled Jennifer's eyes. "I did not realize until this moment how desperate I was to hear some word of praise or appreciation from my family. I can hardly believe such a beautiful, accomplished woman as you admires me."

Jolene covered Jennifer's hand where it lay on the settee. "Your behavior has always been exemplary and you have sacrificed much for this family. I have been ashamed, especially as of late, that I have not carried some of the family burden. I am the oldest, after all. There is an expectation there that I have not lived up to."

"But Little William died of the influenza, and Turner, too. It is no wonder you were unable to concentrate on anything but your own sanity."

Jolene stood and poured herself a cup of tea. "My son's death is a tragedy I will never escape from; however, his memory fills me with joy for the time I had with him. I didn't always feel that way. As I'm sure you were well aware, I was bitter about events in my life. I am no longer," she said and turned to Jennifer. "Turner did not die of the influenza. He hung himself in my rooms with the drapery cords. Alice and I found him just as he died. I was in the carriage ready to leave and realized I needed to change my gloves. Alice and I went back to my rooms . . . and there he was. Swinging and gurgling, and still, I think, able to see us."

Jennifer covered her mouth with her hands. "Oh dear Lord!"

"Did I drive him to it with my accusations that he brought the influenza into our home and killed our son? Perhaps. But ultimately, I did not hang the cord, or put the noose around his neck, or push over the chair stacked on a side table he'd balanced on. Turner killed himself. How desperate must one be to take their own life? Did he suffer from melancholia? Most likely," Jolene said, reseated herself, and looked at Jennifer. "There. I have revealed all of my secrets."

"I am not a person who easily shares her feelings, but I must in the face of your courage," Jennifer said, and walked to the other side of the room, touching the drapery and feeling the chill through the window. Maybe there was some comfort in speaking to an inanimate object such as a pane of glass when making these sorts of confessions, she thought. Looking away instead of into her sister's face gave her some sense of anonymity, even knowing that Jolene could hear everything she said.

"Jeffrey began escorting me to functions or meeting me at the doorway of an event, making it seem as though he and I were always together. I wasn't even aware on some occasions that he'd be riding with Mother and Father and me, and now I believe Mother arranged it to be that way. It was very romantic at first and he told me he could not get enough of me. He would hold my hand while I sat out many dances with other gentlemen as he would say he couldn't bear being parted from me. One of the bank's vice presidents retired and Father told me that he was considering Jeffrey. I approved heartily. Now Father says I asked him to hire Jeffrey, but I didn't. But then . . . well, Jeffrey's behavior stopped being flattering and began to be stifling. Even if I was going to the lady's retiring room, he waited for me. If I stopped and spoke to a friend from Ramsey, Jeffrey would interrupt and tell me that he needed to speak to me. He wanted to know everywhere I went, everyone I spoke to, and everything I did.

"I'd really become tired of it all, and that's when I decided to visit you in Texas. I thought it would cool his passion. We argued over my going and he was very adamant that I shouldn't be traveling alone and that he would be worried about me and that Mother needed me and, well, what he said made me feel very needed and cared for. Looking back, it was not said out of a sense of caring for me, but rather to make me feel guilty. And I did. Feel guilty, that is."

"But you came to the Hacienda anyway."

Jennifer nodded and glanced at her sister. "The day I left was the beginning of the violence. I thought he had resigned himself to the fact that I was going; he had not, however. On the morning I left, he stopped here and walked me into the little room near the parlor. Supposedly to talk privately, and I was hoping that he would apologize for being so high-handed, and even knowing he was not the right man for me, I was hoping he'd kiss me. He hadn't yet, you see, and I'd never really been kissed and well . . ."

"You were curious."

"Yes, I was. I was even thinking that if he kissed me that all his hovering would bother me less and I would be content to marry him. But he was not going to apologize or be nostalgic. He was furious! He said he could not believe I was going through with the trip knowing it displeased him. The next thing I remember, I was on the floor of the room, in horrible pain, Jeffery's face above me. I asked him what happened, and he told me that he hated to punish me but that was the nature of a relationship between a man and a woman. Then he yanked me to my feet and told me to straighten up in a hurry or I would miss my train. I let him lead me out the door and into the family carriage. That is when he kissed me, before he handed me in that is, for all to see."

Jolene groaned and shivered. "What a sickening display that must have been. How were you able to travel?"

"It was a long and arduous trip. And then the Dallas train station was overrun with people trying to escape the influenza and my maid, a silly thing who was no help, ran away from me with half of the cash money I'd brought with me. I barely had enough to hire a wagon, and then the driver left me in the middle of nowhere. Thank God Max came riding by."

"Did you tell Zebidiah any of this? Is that why he is concerned for your safety?"

Jennifer shook her head. "No. When I arrived at the Hacienda and Melinda was so ill, Max asked me to tend Mr. Moran. He was the only one in the bunkhouse and he was in a deep, fever sleep when I lifted my blouse to see if my bruises had faded any more. I was still having some trouble breathing."

"He was not asleep, I presume?"

"No. He was not. He asked me several times when he was well how it had happened. He was very persistent."

"I'm sure he was. He still is where you're concerned. Has he told you he intends to tender his resignation to return to Boston and keep you safe?"

"Yes," Jennifer said. "It is such a sacrifice. I know he cares deeply about the work he does. I hate to see him lose this position, but I am finally able to sleep at night, knowing that he will keep Jeffrey away from me."

"It is interesting, is it not, that Jeffrey wanted *you* to do as he requested, to change for him, and Zebidiah is willing to change *for* you in order to serve you best? One man has his own interests at heart, and one has only yours."

Jennifer blushed. "He is a very busy, important man, though. Once Jeffrey understands that I will not be marrying him, Mr. Moran will move on to other matters."

"Has Rothchild hit you again?"

Jennifer started to shake her head, to deny it, but stopped and looked at her sister's concerned face. "Yes.

We were at the theatre and he took me for air after the first act and pulled me into a closet. He hit me again. Very hard. It was right before I was to come to Washington and he did not want me to go. I told him I wouldn't. But Eliza employed Luther to take my bags on the day before and I told Jeffrey I was meeting friends for a luncheon. I left it for Father to tell him."

"I don't believe that Jeffrey Rothchild will give up easily. He must be furious with you after dinner tonight when Zebidiah made it clear that he would not allow him access to you," Jolene said and joined her at the window. "You must be very careful. This man is dangerous. I know women personally whose husbands hit them regularly and require some violence as a prelude to sex and are inevitably controlling and strict, much more than the restrictions society already places on women. Sadly there is little done. They brutalize their wives and daughters as well, knowing full well that there are few judges who would not think it is within a husband's rights to discipline his wife. I believe Jeffrey Rothchild is such a man."

"But what can he do? Certainly, he will back down now. Certainly he will see that I will not marry him."

"He is a violent man. Do not pretend to be able to reason with him, Jennifer. Stay in your rooms or close to them while Zebidiah travels with me. I have told him I would go alone, or with a servant and be perfectly fine, but he feels obligated to keep the promise he made to Maximillian."

"I will be fine, Jolene," she said and grasped her sister's hands. "But you must go to bed. You are barely standing."

Jennifer went to her mother's room early the next morning. Her eyes were dry and she was tired as she'd not gone to bed until well after midnight and slept fitfully then. Jane Crawford was propped up on pillows, sipping a cup of tea.

"Mother? How are you feeling this morning?" Jennifer asked as she sat down in the chair beside the bed.

"I have nothing to say to you," her mother said with an arched brow. "You are a spoiled girl. It is a miracle that Jeffrey was ever willing to offer for you."

"I am not interested in Jeffrey Rothchild. I will not marry him."

"You are being ridiculous! You must marry him, if he will still have you! Who else will marry you?"

Jennifer took a deep breath. She was determined to be resolved. "I am worried for your health, but you must understand I won't marry him. Do not invite him to dinner. Do not arrange for any meetings between the two of us."

"Freshen my tea, Mildred," Jane said, and sniffed, wrinkling her nose.

Jennifer stood and sat down on the bed beside her mother, who continued to stare out the window. "Mother. Look at me."

Jane took a slow sip of tea. "This is what ungratefulness looks like," she said as her eyes met Jennifer's. "I have put this family, especially my daughters, first, my entire life, and none of you have been appreciative of my efforts. Julia, running away to live on a farm, embarrassing us beyond belief, all because she wanted Jillian as her own daughter! Jolene, losing my grandson and driving her husband to an illness he could not recover from, and marrying a man so beneath her he would not be fit to shine Turner's shoes. And now you! Determined to humiliate your father and me by denying what has been said by the best of Boston's best. The perfect man to carry on our family business, and you say you won't marry him! You will ruin this family!"

Jennifer stared at her mother, the woman's red cheeks and her eyes darting from left to right as if waiting for something or someone to climb over the side of her bed. Why had she not recognized her mother's distance from reality prior to this moment? Why had she doubted her own opinions of events, deferring instead to Jane's warped view of their family history? They were questions that deserved some introspection, but not now. No matter how much her mother's insults cut, she could no longer afford to deal with them emotionally, as she had always done, inevitably reviewing her own behaviors, rather than questioning her mother's version of her daughters' lives. Jennifer refused to give into tears or hysteria, nor would she slink from the inevitable conversation. If she was to heal, if she was to have a chance at happiness, or even some normal life, she had best begin by objecting rather than acquiescing, because after all, something outrageous said often enough is eventually the truth.

"No, Mother. I will not ruin this family as you say and I will not marry Mr. Rothchild. You must come to terms with this. Jolene is leaving in a few days, and I will be planning a small party for her and some of her friends to be held here at Willow Tree. You are ill and I will handle all of the details."

"The idea! You will do no such thing! I will not allow it!"

"It is too late. I have made the invitations and spoken to Cook and Mrs. Gutentide," Jennifer said and turned to Mildred. "Please find me if Mrs. Crawford is in any discomfort."

Mildred eyed her mistress, now shouting her displeasure and pounding her fists into the silk coverlets, and looked back to Jennifer. "Yes, Miss Crawford."

"You are not the mistress of Willow Tree! You are nothing!" Jane shouted and turned to Mildred. "Send a message to Mr. Rothchild. I must speak to him immediately."

Jennifer folded her hands at her waist. "You are ill. I am in charge of Willow Tree for the time being and your care, Mother. Mildred will not be sending any messages to an unmarried man to visit with you in your bedchamber. Get some rest, Mother," she said as she walked toward the door, her heart pounding in her chest.

Chapter Twelve

"THE BANKING LEGISLATION IS CRITICAL. We must have the trust of our fellow citizens if we are to prosper," Jennifer said. Mr. Owens and Mr. Winslow leaned closer, and her father looked at her strangely. Owens, Winslow, and her father were conversing about bank business in regards to proposed regulations, but of course making no mention of their respective businesses' obligations. Jennifer had been reading yearly reports, following the financials in the *Globe*, and listening to members of the Boston bank community for as long as she could remember and was well acquainted with the particulars.

"What did you say, my dear?" Mr. Owens, the vice president of the Massachusetts Bank, asked.

"We must guarantee our depositors' money in some fashion if we are to continue and attract new investors," she said. "Not just today's investor but tomorrow's as well."

"This panic has all been caused by those Argentinians, who don't have the stomach to control their own people. Now they're in the middle of a coup! This will be a disaster for us, mark my words," Mr. Winslow said.

"The Sherman Act is the problem," Mr. Owens said. "Cleveland will be the death of free banking."

"We cannot control anarchy or unrest or poor decisions that we do not make," Jennifer said. "But we must control the outcome."

"How do you propose that, Miss Crawford? We will be taxed and regulated so much we will not be able to turn a profit!"

"We really have no choice, Mr. Owens. I think you all," she said, and stopped to look each man including her father in the eye, "realize something must be done to stabilize commerce and calm nervous investors but you hesitate to act until your tenures as the heads of some of Boston's most elite banks are near to a close. You certainly do not want to be the ones blamed for lower profits."

"Now, Jennifer," her father began.

But Mr. Winslow stopped him and smiled shrewdly. "She does you credit, William, and you despaired of having no sons. I have two extraordinarily lazy ones who do not understand the world of finance nearly as well as Miss Crawford. Perhaps she would consider marrying one of them and explaining to them how commerce works."

"But she is affianced to Rothchild," Mr. Owens said. "What a lucky man he is!"

"He is . . . he is not my fiancé," Jennifer said. "I am not engaged to him."

Zeb watched Jennifer while he stood leaning against the mantel, near enough to listen, but not so close as to be part of their conversation. Her hands shook, and she spoke barely above a whisper, but had the full attention of these clearly powerful and wealthy Bostonians.

"*Humph*," Owens said. "I think some of your investors were looking to see some new blood at your bank, William. There is some talk behind the scenes that some of your books are not up to snuff. But if Miss Crawford has declined his offer . . ."

Jennifer straightened as if she'd been slapped, and her father reached an arm around her as he replied. "We have uncovered a clerk who is challenged by columns of figures. We have found him new tasks at the bank more to his abilities. The books are in order."

"My wife's cousin's son cannot add or subtract sufficiently to count stacks of one dollar notes. I finally had to fire him. Christmas visits with my wife's family will be interesting," Winslow said.

William Crawford directed the men to the buffet laid out with pastries and cheeses. Jennifer turned to Zeb.

"You are white as my hanky. What has happened?" Zeb asked.

"Owens heard our books were not up to snuff," she said. "I am concerned that rumors have begun."

"Your father smoothed it over nicely, I thought."

"Do you think they were convinced?"

"It is that critical?"

She nodded. "Yes. Banks have closed their doors on less."

"You think Rothchild is doing this?"

"Absolutely. He already threatened it."

"I think this party for Jolene proves exactly the opposite of what Rothchild may be saying. Your sister adds her considerable skills, and your father and yourself looking and sounding competent and confident, undoubtedly belies Rothchild's descriptions, which I imagine are that you are a family in crisis."

Jennifer nodded. "Yes. That is what he would be saying, although it would be just a word dropped here or there. He would be subtle and believable."

"And you are believable as well. Jolene, for her part, has not denied that Max is considering a run for the presidency."

"The presidency? I did not know that Max had those aspirations."

"I don't think he does, but when the woman over there in the green dress said that the next thing Max would be eyeing is the executive mansion, Jolene just smiled and said nothing. Of course, now the room is buzzing with gossip that Jolene Crawford Shelby's husband is considering a run for the presidency. It doesn't hurt the family reputation."

"Mother thinks it does. She says politicians are crass."

Zeb smiled. "She's right, but they are also powerful men with the ability to bestow favor and displeasure even in the business world."

"I am not sure if my comments were well received by Owens and Winslow. Women are not welcome amongst bankers, except, of course, for Mrs. Ebbitt. There she is," Jennifer pointed out with a nod to a frail-looking white-haired woman speaking to several men and women. "I was very glad she accepted my invitation."

"The pale woman in the black dress? She looks quite elderly," he said.

"She must be near seventy years old. She still goes every day to the offices at Ebbitt Bank," she said and turned to him. "Mrs. Ebbitt is famous here in Boston. She was a renowned debutante in her day from what I've been told and married Mr. Ebbitt, the son of the founder of Ebbitt Bank and Loan. He was no more than forty when he died from an insufficiency of the heart, and Mrs. Ebbitt's children were not of age. She took over her husband's position at the bank, and as she was the majority stockholder, there was little to be done about it by the board of directors. She kept the bank afloat and prosperous until her son was able to take over. Although rumors are that she still runs the company and he is merely a figurehead."

"She is to be admired," Zeb said, and leaned close. "But there is nothing she has done that you would not be able to. Your father is a fool if he does not recognize that."

Jennifer shook her head. "No. I am not clever enough for that sort of thing."

"So you choose to believe what your mother has told you all these years."

"I . . . I don't have the background or the courage to do what Mrs. Ebbitt has done."

"You are already doing it, Jennifer."

She turned her head sharply. "No. I'm merely—" But she was cut off by her father.

"Come along, Jennifer," he said. "Owens is insisting you join in the conversation we are having with some investors, and I think we have managed to quiet Rothchild's rumors. What an excellent idea this party was, my dear. Jolene is at her best, even in her delicate condition, and you are giving our partners, and our competitors, confidence. You know as well as I that if one Boston bank goes down, it is only bad news for all those remaining. Come. They are waiting."

* * *

Zeb waited near the stairs as Jennifer and her father said good night to the last guest. Crawford stayed to give the butler some instruction, and Jennifer walked to Zeb. Her eyes were shining and she was smiling.

"Quite a successful soiree you've hosted, Miss Crawford."

"It was, was it not? Cook outdid herself with the food, and father was in his glory with Jolene to show off," she said. "Yes. It was a roaring success!"

"You had no small part in that. I watched you in conversation with a variety of people. They were waiting to hear your comments and leaning in close to hear your every word. You had Boston's banking elite hanging on every word."

Crawford stopped at his daughter's side. "I am going to check on your mother. Good night, Jennifer. Well done. You are going to your rooms?" he asked with a sideways glance at Zeb.

"I am coming very shortly, Father. I am exhausted," she said and watched him climb the stairs before turning back to Zeb.

"I am leaving tomorrow, very early, to escort your sister to Washington. I will be back Monday morning at the latest but I may be back as early as Sunday afternoon. Please tell me you will remember to stay here at Willow Tree until Sunday evening when either I or Calving Billings arrives to escort you to the Hospital Soiree," Zeb said.

"I will," she said. "I told my father that Jeffrey was ill and couldn't attend this evening. I never sent him an invitation. Father thinks I have judged him harshly and I will damage his reputation in the banking community if I am not careful."

"He has hit you, I'm sure of it, and I suspect he is doing something nefarious at the bank. I will be happy to damage more than his reputation."

"Perhaps that will not be necessary. Maybe he will have some understanding now that I am not going to marry him. Perhaps we can just be polite to each other and go our separate ways."

Zeb laid his hands on her shoulders. "No, Jennifer. He is not the type of man to give up. Trust me on this. He will not quit until he has hurt you in some way even more than he already has. Promise me you will be very careful. Promise me you will not leave Willow Tree until I've returned, or unless you are with Calvin Billings."

"I promise."

He touched his lips to hers and felt her breath against his mouth. "I will not be satisfied until I am back in Boston and able to see to your welfare."

She looked into his eyes. "You have no obligation to me. We are not courting, or affianced. Why are you doing this?"

"Let us worry about that later after you are safe. After your secrets are out or solved."

Jennifer stepped back and searched his face. "I will see you on Sunday or Monday, then. I must go up now, even though I'd prefer not to."

"Yes. You should go up before I kiss you and do not want to leave."

"Good night, Zebidiah."

"Good night, Jenny. You will be careful?"

She nodded and turned to hurry up the steps.

* * *

Jennifer kept to her rooms both days, other than checking on her mother every few hours. Jane was in so much pain that she'd not left her bed for three days and was willingly taking the laudanum that Dr. Roderdeck had prescribed. When Jennifer did leave her rooms, she found Luther lurking nearby.

"Luther," she said finally. "Are you following me? I don't think that is necessary within the confines of Willow Tree. How are you getting your other duties performed if you are constantly in my attendance?"

"I work through the night, Miss Crawford. Do not worry about me. I'm hoping to better myself, and Mr. Moran told me if all goes well here, he may have a position in Washington for me, working for him."

"You would be interested in working with Mr. Moran in Washington?"

He nodded. "He told me I would start out by getting him to and from his offices every day and other places he needs to go, that he doesn't have a moment to spare to hire carriages and such. He said I'd be reading and learning while I'm waiting for him and that he would see to my education." He continued softly, "That is if he still has his job when this danger to you has passed."

"He will have his job, Luther," she said. "I think the danger *has* passed, and the senator values Mr. Moran's counsel. I think he will be back in Washington within the week once he has seen that all is calm here."

"I hope all is calm, but I'll still do as Mr. Moran has told me to do."

Clearly those around her thought that she was still in danger, and now this drama was disrupting schedules and lives. How she wished she'd never encouraged Jeffrey Rothchild all those months ago, even believing Jolene that anyone could have been fooled. Even knowing that there were no signs early on, that she didn't have an inkling that he was not honorable, that he was, in fact, violent. She'd spent her life avoiding others' notice, staying clear of her mother's attention, as that only brought embarrassment and pain. How she hated being center stage! She much preferred to be part of the silent observers, content to follow the tides rather than make one.

Jennifer left Eliza laying out her clothes for the Hospital Soiree and mending her pale blue satin slippers that matched the Dutch blue and cream watered silk gown that she would be wearing that evening, to check on her mother's condition.

"You are sitting up," Jennifer said with a smile when she went in her mother's room. "You must be feeling considerably better."

"Where is my bath, Mildred? Did you call for it?" Jane demanded.

"I will check on it for you, ma'am," Mildred replied and scurried from the room.

Jennifer hurried to her mother's side as she rose from the edge of the bed on unsteady legs. "Take your time, Mother. You have been abed and in pain."

Jane shook off Jennifer's hand on her elbow. "I need no assistance from you. Leave. I must prepare for the Hospital Soiree."

"What? No! You are in no condition to go out, Mother," she said, and watched as her mother wobbled to the end of the mattress and grabbed the bedpost to steady herself. "You will make yourself ill and your surgery is this week. Surely Dr. Roderdeck would not approve."

"That quack does not determine my social calendar. I have never missed a Hospital Soiree and don't intend to!"

"Father is still at the Banking Association meeting held at his club and told me he will meet me at the soiree. Calvin and Eugenia Billings are coming here to take me with them."

"Don't be ridiculous," Jane said as Mildred opened the door and ushered in young men and women carrying a tub and buckets of water. "You will ride with me in the Crawford carriage. There is no reason to demean yourself by arriving with *those* people."

"But Mother." Jennifer shook her head. "You do not understand . . . you do not know . . . I have promised—"

"Promised whom?" Jane interjected. "You would disregard the needs of your own mother to humiliate me this way? I am ill, as you constantly remind me. Can't you have some pity on your mother?"

"But . . . I—"

"Out with you now. I want to take my bath in privacy and comfort. Stoke that fire up, boy," Jane directed one of the young men now dumping steaming buckets of water into the copper tub. "Strangers come in and use our bathing room. I will no longer bathe there."

"Strangers?" Jennifer asked and looked at Mildred, who would not meet her eye.

"Out!" Jane said and pointed to the door. "Out with all of you. Mildred will stay and assist me."

Jennifer thought about her promise to Zeb to attend with the Billingses. But surely he would understand that her mother would need assistance, and hadn't she just told Luther that the danger had passed? She would ride in the family carriage with her mother to the Hospital Soiree and have Luther ride up front with the driver. Jennifer hurried to her room to write a note to Jolene's sister-in-law Eugenia to tell her she would meet her at the soiree and that she would be riding with her mother and father in the family carriage. Jennifer thought briefly about the small lie that her father would be with her, but she dreaded the possibility that Calvin would play hero and insist that they see her to the Parker House Hotel. He would be mollified if he thought Father would attend her and Mother and she could forego the inevitable scene if the Billingses arrived at Willow Tree. She would have Luther with her in any case, and who would bother her when in his company?

* * *

Jolene and Melinda Shelby were safely deposited with Max, who hugged the two of them as if he had not seen them for years instead of the three weeks they were away. Melinda went running to find her puppy, and Zeb watched as Jolene and Max stared into each other's eyes, holding their hands between them, as they whispered. It made him think of Jennifer, and the soft kiss she'd given him just yesterday.

Jolene kissed Max on the mouth and swept away up the staircase, servants hauling luggage behind her. "Thank you, Zebidiah, for getting us home safely and honoring your promise to Maximillian. Now please return to Boston to guard my sister."

"Guard her sister?" Max asked after he'd ushered Zeb into his library.

"I'm tendering my resignation, Max. It's been an honor serving you and working for you, but I've made a promise that I have to keep. There's one train from Washington to Boston tomorrow and I'll be on it. I'm more sorry than I can say that I'll be unable to stay and help you pick a new chief of staff but I haven't any choice."

"Sit down," Max said as he poured them each a glass of bourbon. "You are not resigning. If you have to keep a promise, then take whatever time you need, but you're not resigning. A young man from that Jesuit school, Georgetown College, showed up at the office looking for work. I liked the look of him and hired him on the spot. He's bright and will manage until you return and teach him how to wrangle a calf or a senator. Do what you have to do now."

Zeb stared at him, willing himself not to do violence with the retelling and hoping that Jennifer forgave him when she found out he'd told Max her story. He could no longer keep it bottled up inside. He was sick to the stomach with worry and he needed a man's opinion and advice.

"He's beating her, Max," he said finally. "Rothchild is hitting Jennifer."

Max leaned forward across the desk. "He's beating her?" he repeated. "Tell me."

Zeb told him about seeing her in the bunkhouse at the Hacienda and in the music room at Willow Tree, and touching her side as they danced on the night of Max's election celebration. He told him Rothchild's reaction to his interference and about O'Brien's injuries, and the message she'd carried.

"Jennifer has not come out and told me but I believe Rothchild is stealing from the bank somehow and she has uncovered his methods. Her father doesn't believe her. Her mother is sick in both mind and body, and Jennifer is terrified. I told her I would guard her safety while she straightens out the bank's issues, which she must do secretly as she has told me that any rumor of this nature could shutter the bank."

"She is knowledgeable about the workings of the bank?"

Zeb nodded. "Very. She doesn't give herself credit, but she is. They are all at the mercy of the mother, who makes a shrew appealing."

"I feel personally responsible for Jennifer as she's my wife's unmarried sister and the father lets the mother treat them with an unnatural cruelty. I am in your debt for handling this for me," Max said. "Does Calvin know?"

"I did not tell him any particulars, but yes. He's escorting Jennifer to a soiree tomorrow evening if I have not returned and he understands the danger she may be in. Rothchild is not a man who will ever back down, and he manipulates the mother and has played her the fool publically."

"You will make sure to kill him?"

"I will not say anything to you on that subject. I will not have the United States senator from Texas as a witness in a murder trial. Anyway, you can't have a chief of staff who has been charged with murder, and I can't let the particulars come out if it will damage Jennifer or her work."

"You would go to jail before telling a judge he was beating her or robbing her family's bank, or his part in this O'Brien girl's injuries?"

Zeb stared out the long window. He surely did not want to go to jail but he would, he supposed, if it came to it. He would not have Jennifer threatened any longer, whatever it took.

"Your silence is damning."

"I'll handle it, Max."

"I'll be happy to go with you back to Boston, you know."

"I know you would, but I can't allow it. I can't let you risk that you will be involved with something that is detrimental to your career. In any case," Zeb said, and met his eyes, "Jennifer Crawford is *my* concern. I will see to her safety and happiness."

"Ahhh," Max said and folded his hands in front of him, taking a moment before finally looking Zeb in the eye. "She may need time. When this is over, I mean. She may not be able to just slough it off. Jolene wasn't, and she is the strongest woman I've ever met. There's an ugliness in that family that can't be dismissed quickly. You'll need to be patient."

"I will give her anything, including time. Anything she asks for or wants."

Chapter Thirteen

ZEB SLEPT SOUNDLY AFTER A meal of his cook's beef stew and bread, still hot and yeasty from the oven. He dressed with care in a formal black suit, not the tuxedo with the satin collar, but still fancy enough for a society dinner when he arrived in Boston. He had his gun belt on under his jacket, something he'd not done since arriving in the capital, and a knife in his boot. He'd shaved with care and looked around his sleeping room as it might be the last he saw of it for quite some time, if ever, if things didn't fall his way. He arrived at the station early, bought two newspapers and an orange, and boarded the train. He would arrive an hour before the Hospital Soiree started, leaving him plenty of time to arrive at Willow Tree and relieve Luther. The train's rhythmic chug lulled him to nap, his feet propped up on the empty seat across from him.

He sat up with a start when the sight of Jennifer's face in his dreams became a nightmare as she opened her mouth in a scream. But it was just a child crying a few seats behind him. He shook his head and tried to concentrate on his newspaper but was soon lost in thoughts of Jennifer Crawford. She was reserved and introverted, and it must have been quite a burden for her to put herself out in such a public way as she was doing, he thought as he watched the passing scenery. He wondered if she was thinking of him right now as he was thinking of her.

Suddenly, the train lurched. He grabbed his seat handles and could hear the screech of wheels breaking on the track. Cases fell from the luggage rack overhead, nearly missing the woman with the crying child. The car swayed, and a man fell into the aisle, sliding along the floor past Zeb. The train stopped with a high-pitched whine of metal against metal and clanging as its cars banged against one another in succession.

Zeb helped the man on the floor to his feet and looked around at his fellow passengers, mostly white-faced with fear and some of the women visibly trembling. A conductor came through the door to the car at that moment.

"There's a herd of cows on the tracks ahead. Engineer done killed a couple. We have to get the carcasses off the tracks now," he called out as he went down the aisle to the next car.

"Damnation," Zeb said under his breath as the other passengers shouted questions or spoke hurriedly to one another. He looked at his pocket watch. This mess was going to make his arrival very close. He tried to console himself that Luther was there and Calvin would be escorting her, but he couldn't shake the feeling that something was wrong. That Jennifer was in danger.

* * *

"You must go back to bed," Jennifer said, holding her mother's arm as she walked slowly down the stairs. "You are in pain."

"Hush!" Jane said through white, trembling lips. "I am going and you will not stop me! I am not a child!"

Jennifer let out a held breath and loosened her grip on her mother's arm when they reached the white marble tiled floor of the foyer. Her mother was holding on to the bannister and taking deep, slow breaths.

"Please," Jennifer said. "I beg of you. Stop this foolishness. You are in no condition to leave Willow Tree."

"Oh, yes, I am," Jane said and straightened her back. "I am going to the Hospital Soiree!"

She followed her mother over to where Bellings stood with a thick coat.

"Button it, Bellings," Jane said with closed eyes.

"Yes, of course, Mrs. Crawford," he said, as if he buttoned his mistress's wrap every day, and glanced at Jennifer.

Bellings placed Jennifer's royal blue cape, trimmed with an ermine collar, over her bare shoulders. She was feeling sick to her stomach, thinking about her mother and the soiree and Rothchild and the note she'd sent Calvin and Eugenia.

"Where is Luther?" she asked Bellings as she gave a last tug on her white kid gloves. "He will be riding with the driver this evening."

"I do not know, Miss Jennifer. Let me check on him for you," he said, and turned to a young man waiting attentively in the hallway.

"Who is this Luther person and why is he riding with us? Who is driving the carriage this evening, Bellings?" Jane asked.

"Jasper, ma'am."

A young servant walked up to Bellings and spoke softly into his ear. Bellings looked at Jennifer. "Luther is . . . unavailable, miss. Is there anyone else you'd like me to call?"

"Unavailable? That's impossible. I spoke to him this afternoon. He knew what time we were departing. Where is he?"

"He is indisposed," Bellings began, but the young servant interrupted.

"He's drunk, miss. Can barely stand on two feet, and singing songs at the top of his voice."

"Drunk? Dismiss him immediately, Bellings. We do not tolerate servants that are drunkards," Jane said.

"Where is he?" Jennifer asked. "Take me to him."

"You will not be in company with a drunken manservant, Jennifer! I forbid it!"

"I must speak to him, Mother. Wait here. I'll only be a moment." Jennifer followed the young servant to the kitchen entrance and heard shouting from belowstairs. She hurried down the steps.

Mrs. Gutentide and Cook were leaning over Luther, who sat on the floor, his back propped up against the wall. They were making him drink from a ladle. "Come on, now, Luther, boy. Drink this. It will make you feel better."

"Mrs. Gutentide! What is the matter with him?" Jennifer asked.

She straightened and hurried to Jennifer's side. "He's drunk, miss, I'm sorry to say."

"I don't think that's it," Cook said. "This boy never has more than one or two pints, and with that new fancy job he's getting, I don't see him risking everything on drink."

"What do you think it is then?" Jennifer asked and knelt down. "Luther? Can you hear me?"

An older man knelt on the other side. “Luther, boy! Wake up!”

Luther opened his eyes.

The old man tapped the sides of his face. “What did you drink, boy? Where was ya?”

Luther shook his head. “Stopped at The Tavern for some stew and a pint. Don’t remember much after that.”

The old man looked at Mrs. Gutentide and Jennifer. “Somebody put something in his drink, I be thinking. I saw him leave the kitchens no more than an hour ago with the kettle that needed forged. It would have been a half hour ’til he could even get to The Tavern from the metalworks.”

“And then ten minutes’ walk here,” Mrs. Gutentide said. “There was no time for him to drink much at all!”

Jennifer’s stomach turned over. Luther was clearly unable to ride with her and there was a suggestion that he had been drugged. Bellings appeared and helped Jennifer to her feet.

“Mrs. Crawford is insisting that you come upstairs at once, miss. She is most impatient to leave.”

“Of course,” Jennifer said and turned to the steps. “Please call Dr. Roderdeck to attend Luther.”

Jennifer rushed across the foyer to where her mother stood at the door. She was shouting.

“I will not stand for this disrespect! I will not stand for it!”

"Calm yourself, Mother. You will exhaust yourself. Come. Let me escort you up to Mildred. She will help you get into bed."

"Absolutely not! I am going to the Hospital Soiree whether you come with me or not. Call for the carriage, Bellings."

"I am not sure this is a good idea," she said, knowing that her mother would not understand, or perhaps even care, what she meant.

Bellings opened the door, and Jennifer followed her mother onto the portico and down the steps to the drive where the carriage was pulling up. The old man who had tended Luther jumped down from the driver's seat. "Luther begged me to go with you. Are you in some danger, miss?" he asked.

She looked at her mother, climbing into the carriage with Bellings's assistance. She turned back to the old man. "You are Mr. Hadley, correct?" she asked.

He nodded.

"Is that Jasper at the reins? It doesn't look like him," Jennifer said.

"Jasper's a bit under the weather, miss. This here's Nelson. He's new."

"Jennifer!" her mother called. "Get in this carriage. We will be late if we do not leave immediately."

"This seems to be a series of most unfortunate incidents, and there could be some danger, Mr. Hadley," Jennifer said and laid a hand on his arm. "We are only going a short distance into town proper to the Parker House Hotel, but be attentive."

"Yes, miss," he said and climbed up beside the driver.

"Whatever have you been doing, Jennifer? I am feeling quite restored having gotten some fresh air. Tell him to drive, Bellings," her mother said through the open door.

Everything she had promised Zeb she would not do or would not let happen had occurred, and she was at a loss as to what she could have done differently, other than perhaps digging in her heels and not getting in the carriage without Luther. But could she allow her mother to travel even this short distance alone? Jennifer climbed into the carriage and settled her cloak around herself, listening to her mother complain that if they arrived late it would be her fault. She looked out the window and scanned the buildings they were passing.

"This is not the way to the Parker House Hotel," she said, and began to give into the panic she had been barely able to contain. She banged her fist on the ceiling of the carriage and shouted, "Where are we going?"

"Settle yourself, Jennifer. What a spectacle you are making!"

"Mother! We are not going to the Parker House Hotel!"

"Of course, we are not, Jennifer."

"Where are we going, Mother? What have you done?" she whispered, and felt the blood drain from her face. She heard shouting from the driver's seat and saw something tumble past her window. The carriage careened and she hung on to the edge of the seat trying to see out her window. There was a man in the gutter, just now up on all fours and shaking his head. *Hadley!*

* * *

Zeb finally climbed down from the steps and walked to the head of the engine of the train. He surveyed the mess and watched as men pulled and pushed the remains of a cow's carcass off of the tracks. Two other men were using tools on the train's wheels.

"Nearly done here," one of the men working on the train said. "Get the passengers back in the cars."

"We're not going to be able to move at full speed, I'm a feared. We can only do so much until we get this engine back to the yard."

Zeb turned and walked back to his car. He told a few of the other men there waiting with their families what he'd heard. "So we'll be underway soon but we won't be going very fast."

The next two hours were spent staring out the window onto the dark landscape, trying to shake the feeling that something was terribly wrong. Something that felt like it could not be fixed.

* * *

"Tell me, Mother. What have you done?"

"I did no more than what any mother would do. Someone must control this family's destiny. Your father certainly won't! He never has!"

Jennifer swallowed, real fear creeping up her back and around her gut, making her knees shake and her palms sweat. "It is not too late, Mother. Tell me what you have planned."

"I can hardly take credit, Jennifer," Jane said with a smile. "Your fiancé is really very clever and has orchestrated a lovely evening for the two of you. An evening to reconcile your differences. You must do as he says, dear. It will only hurt for a short while." Her mother looked out the window of the carriage, a wistful, faraway look on her face. "Rothchild is very manly. I'm sure you'll be well satisfied; however, you must take care not to show it. Men do prefer a docile wife."

Bile rose in Jennifer's throat and she leaned back against the cushions of the well-appointed Crawford carriage. Her mother had arranged for her to be taken sexually by a violent man. How absolutely appalling, and yet worst of all, she was not surprised when it was revealed. Did she really believe her own excuse that there was no risk? No. Of course she had not. She had known Rothchild was a dangerous man, and she was in his sights. But she had not truly believed Jolene, had she? She had not wanted to believe Zeb, either. She'd walked right into Rothchild's dastardly plan, but that did not mean she would go down without a fight. She would fight with her dying breath.

The carriage came to a stop and the door opened. "My fiancée! How lovely you look this evening," Rothchild said. "Get out of the carriage."

Jennifer pulled off her gloves, laying them on the seat beside her. Without them, she would be able to scratch him. She could bite him or kick him when it came to it. For now, if she made him reach in for her inside the carriage there would be a scuffle and her mother could be hurt. Fleetingly, it occurred to her that perhaps she should quit caring for her mother but sense prevailed, if not love or like, and Jennifer got out of the carriage on her own.

"What do you want, Jeffrey? There are people expecting me at the Hospital Soiree," she said with a shaking voice as the carriage pulled away.

"Perhaps," he replied, "but they will not know where to look for you, now will they?"

She looked around then and realized she did not recognize the street. They were not in the neighborhood that Jeffrey lived in or anywhere she'd ever been before. "Where are we?"

"We are just a few doors away from privacy and a large bed. Come dear. We'll make this all painless. There is no need to be frightened. Just do as you're told."

"No," she said. "No. I won't. I won't do as I'm told." She turned then to run, but Jeffrey had her arm and pulled her sharply around.

She tried to pull away from his iron grip but his fingers would not release her. She looked up at him and he smiled at her.

"Are you done yet?"

Jennifer screamed as loudly as she could. When Rothchild clamped a hand around her mouth, she bit down on his finger, and he took a wide roundhouse swing with an open palm, landing a slap on her cheek and the side of her head. She was stunned but screamed again, tasting blood from her lip as she did. She saw a door open a few houses away.

"Help!" she screamed. "Help me!"

Rothchild grabbed her around the waist and dragged and carried her to a set of steps. He pulled her along and released one hand while he fumbled with a key at the door. Jennifer shoved at him wildly and slipped by him. He caught her by the hair just a few steps away and pulled her up the steps again, losing a slipper as she went, and through the door. He locked it behind him and dropped the key in his pocket.

She was shaking and terrified. There was no one to help her but herself. "What is this place?"

"This place is my secretary Mr. Jefferson's humble home. It is not as plush and accommodating as a hotel room, where I'd planned to spend our wedding trip, but it will do. There is a bed upstairs with clean sheets and a bottle of wine for you to settle your nerves, but after this ridiculous display of independence you will not have it so easy, my dear Jennifer. You are going to bend over one of

Jefferson's wooden kitchen chairs like the whore that you are and have your maidenhead breached. I am quite ready to perform several times, as I have not visited my mistress for weeks in anticipation of this event."

Jennifer gagged, shook her head, and began to back up. She turned and ran down the dark hallway into a kitchen, lit only by a sliver of light coming through a window. She could hear Rothchild laughing and following her. Her hand swept across a wooden counter, dishes and cups clattering to the floor until she touched what she'd been looking for. She waited there then, her back up against the counter, glass from the broken dishes cutting through her slipper and the skin of her bare foot with each step or movement.

"I see you are much anticipating the kitchen chair," Rothchild said with a laugh, putting his jacket on the table and rolling up his sleeves. "Drop your skirts now, Jennifer. There is nowhere to run."

She drew a shaking hand up her side, watching his movements in the dim light, and picked at the buttons fastening her skirts to the bodice. One gave way and she pulled at another. "I can't get them to unbutton," she said and swiped at the tears rolling down her face.

"Use both hands, Jennifer. There is no need to prolong your misery. Let us get this first coupling out of the way as it will most likely not be pleasurable for me and I'm certain it will not be pleasurable for you."

"I've cut my other hand on a broken dish. It is bleeding badly."

"You poor, dear," he said and walked toward her. "Do not get any blood on your skirt, Jennifer. We will be arriving late at the soiree. There will be little doubt then that we will be marrying when the men smell the sex on you. Even your father. He will know, and if he doesn't, we will endeavor to lead him and others into a room where he will find you on your knees with your mouth taking the full length of my cock. You will have practiced a few times before we arrive so you will know exactly what to do. We'll be married by tomorrow noon."

* * *

Zeb hurried from the station the minute the train rattled to a stop. He hailed a carriage for hire and told the driver to take him directly to the soiree. He fingered his gun in its holster and knew with some clarity that if Jennifer had made it to the hotel, she would be relatively safe. Danger lay ahead if she hadn't arrived. He told the driver to take him to Willow Tree instead, as fast as he could drive. He jumped from the carriage, pounded on the door, and waited until Bellings opened it.

"Mr. Moran. It is good to have you back at Willow Tree."

"Where is Miss Crawford?" Zeb asked in a rush as he stepped into the foyer.

"She's gone to the Hospital Soiree with her mother, Mr. Moran. She left more than thirty minutes ago."

"Was Luther with her?"

"No. Very unusual. We believe Luther was drugged, sir."

"Moran!" Zeb heard through the open door.

"Miss Crawford's been taken!" an older man shouted as he limped up the front steps, a handkerchief over a large, bleeding gash in his head.

Bellings shouted to a young servant to get Dr. Roderdeck from Luther's quarters as Zeb helped the man into a chair and knelt in front of him. "We're going to get you to a doctor, but please tell what you know. Where is Miss Crawford?"

"I rode up with the driver. Weren't Jasper. New man instead. I asked the man where we were going when I seen we weren't going to the hotel. He hit me in the head with something heavy, knocked me off the bench, and kept going."

Bellings handed the man a glass of water, and he drank every bit down, making Zeb want to yank it out of his hand, take him by his homespun collar, and shake him until he told him the the last place he'd seen Jennifer. The old man handed off the glass.

"I got pushed out at Green near Third Street. By the time I could stand up, the carriage was gone but I saw him turn onto Fifth Street. I hightailed it back here for help."

"They've taken her, haven't they?" O'Brien said as she hurried across the foyer, followed by her father. "Where is she?"

Zeb stood. "Miss O'Brien?"

"I heard Luther was drugged. He told me he was to look out for Jennifer, and then I heard he could not go with her this evening."

"Hadley says he saw the carriage carrying Miss Crawford turn onto Fifth," Bellings said.

"Fifth near Green? Yes?" She looked at Zeb. "Father has made recent inquiries for me. Rothchild's secretary lives on Fifth. Jefferson. Bernard Jefferson is his name."

Zeb ran out of the house to the carriage still waiting. Thomas O'Brien grabbed his arm.

"I have a horse saddled. It will be faster. I'll leave Kathleen and Sean here with my man. Hadley and I will follow in the carriage. Go! Go! Time is wasting!"

"I don't know Boston! Where is Fifth?"

Thomas gave him hurried directions as he climbed into the carriage with Hadley.

Zeb ran down the steps just as a young boy came around the side of Willow Tree riding a massive beast of a horse. The boy slid down the horse's side and handed the reins off to Zeb, barely in the saddle and stirrups and already kicking the horse into motion.

"Yaw!" he shouted. He ran the horse down city streets, carriages pulling out of his way and one horseless carriage blowing a horn, making his mount rear up on hind legs. He got the horse under control and saw the street ahead that he was looking for, making a sharp, dangerous turn as fast as the horse would take it. He thundered down the next street, praying that he was not too late, that he would see his Jenny, rescue her and keep her safe for as long as they lived. But there were no guarantees as he was well aware, and he steeled himself for whatever heartbreak that might be ahead this night.

He followed the final direction Hadley had shouted to him and turned onto Fifth Street, slowing his mount and peering into the shadows of trees down a long avenue, with no idea which door Jennifer was behind. A man and woman stood on a stoop, he could see from the gas streetlight, arguing, the woman shaking a finger in the man's face.

"I'm searching for a woman. She's in trouble. Have you seen anyone while you were out of doors?" he called to them.

The woman pulled a wrap tightly around herself and hurried down stone steps. "Yes! There was a woman screaming for help when I put me cat out just a few minutes ago. I've been trying to get my husband to look for her."

Zeb jumped down and grabbed the woman's shoulders. "Where? Where did you see her? Do you know which house belongs to Bernard Jefferson?"

The woman shook her head. "They went up the steps of one of the houses right there," she said and pointed down the street. "But I'm not sure which one. I ran back into my house for my husband and didn't see where they went."

Zeb hurried down the street, looking and listening for anything that might tell him where to look. Something blue caught his eye as the moonlight cut through the trees, giving off a silver reflection. He ran up the steps and picked up a shoe. A woman's shoe, covered in pale blue satin, new but scuffed and torn along the side and heel. Jennifer!

Zeb ran full tilt at the door, ripping some of the frame away from the brick. "Jennifer!" he shouted. "Jennifer! Where are you?" He ran at the door again, throwing his shoulder and side at the wood near where the frame was loose.

* * *

Jennifer blinked away tears and tried not to focus on the vile description that Jeffrey had just given. To think her father would see her on her . . . *Stop! Stop allowing Jeffrey to frighten you when you need your wits about you*, she said to herself. *Save yourself!* She let the tears tumble then and dropped her shoulders, acquiescing with her body to his pronouncements and praying that he would come just a few more steps closer. She had but one chance and she would not lose it by giving into the emotion and terror that she was feeling. Let him think he had the upper hand as he always had! Let him think she was weak and cowardly!

Jeffrey took a step closer and undid the button she'd been struggling with, letting her skirts fall around her knees. He ran his hand gently through her hair as she held her breath, not daring to look him in the eye. With one smooth motion he wrapped his right arm around her, pulled her close, twisting the fingers of his left hand in her hair, pulling back sharply on her head. "Get ready, my dear."

Jennifer welcomed the pain as he yanked her head back, growled low in her chest, and bared her teeth at him. "Never!" she shouted and brought the cooking knife up from her petticoats in a swift motion, the tip entering Rothchild's side. She met his eyes then, now shocked, as he stumbled away from her, looking down at his stomach where the knife was buried to the hilt and his ripped shirt was turning crimson.

"Jennifer! Where are you?" she heard.

"Zeb! Zeb! I'm here!" she shouted, as she stumbled out of her petticoats and skirt, and pushed her way past Rothchild as he pulled the knife out of his body.

Jennifer went down the hall just as Zeb came through the door, landing on the broken wood of the frame and jumping to his feet.

"Jennifer!"

"Help me," she said, then crumbled to her knees, tears streaming down her face.

But Zeb was not looking at her. His eyes and gun were trained on Jeffrey Rothchild as he staggered out of the kitchen behind Jennifer, raising his hand holding a bloody knife and staring at her back. As his arm began its descent, the sudden quiet was broken by a gunshot from Zeb's pistol. Rothchild pitched wildly and landed, eyes open in a dead stare, beside Jennifer.

Jennifer gasped out a few horrified breaths as she looked into the face of her tormentor, just inches from her, blood pooling in his mouth, running down his cheek, and dribbling onto her chemise caught under the weight of his soon-to-be dead body. And then everything in her world went black.

Chapter Fourteen

Six Months Later

ZEB HANDED HIS HAT TO Max's butler and turned to Bella. "I am starved," he said to his sister. "I don't remember eating anything all day."

"You need to gain two stone to begin to look like the brother I know and love. Your cook is not lacking, though, I've found."

"I'm very glad of your company for this upcoming week," he said and pulled her arm through his as he led her down the hallway to Max and Jolene's dining room. He could hear laughter and conversation already, and Max's booming voice above all.

"It is no wonder!" Bella admonished. "You work twelve hours a day and nearly fall into bed from your exhaustion. That poor young man, Luther, begins before you in the morning. When one's stoic brother writes that he's adrift, it is time to speak to him face to face. I got your letter and went directly to my room to begin packing."

Zeb squeezed her hand where it lay on his arm. "I did not mean to be dramatic."

She stopped and looked up at her brother, now sporting tired lines around his mouth, set grimly as she was unfortunately becoming accustomed to seeing. His shirt collar was a tad loose, and even though he was looking at her, she sensed he was not seeing her, that his mind was far away with a woman he'd not spoken to in nearly six months.

"You're breaking my heart, Zebidiah," she whispered. "You've mostly been a man of few words, but you were never sad like you are now. You are so unhappy and I'm afraid I am unable to help you."

"I'm fine, Bella," he said and smiled down at her. "I'm much better for your being here."

"So this is the sister you've been hiding from us," Max said as he came down the hallway.

"Senator Shelby," Bella said with a smile and held out her hand. "It is a pleasure to finally meet you."

"A Southern belle!" Max said. "I've forgotten how lovely a woman sounds when she hails from Atlanta.

Don't tell my bride, though. Those Bostonians think they are the most perfect women, but then I do, too!"

Bella laughed, and Zeb followed Max, now leading his sister through the dining room doors. He saw Jolene stand from her chair and walk to Bella with a welcoming smile. He looked around the room, hoping Melinda had been allowed to stay up and eat with the adults. But his gaze did not travel far. His eyes were arrested by a woman. The most beautiful, delicate woman he'd ever known. Would ever know. He felt tears at the back of his eyes at the sight of her and concentrated on getting his emotions under control. Jennifer stood, facing him across the table, her lip trembling.

"Hello, Zeb," she whispered.

"Miss Crawford," he said when he found his voice. He did not take his eyes from her, as she was once again seated. Wishing to drink in her likeness, commit it to a permanent memory, so that her vision in his head was fresh and new when he lay down to sleep that night. She was wearing a daring dark green dress, low-cut and matching the exact color of her eyes. He was still standing when Max stood and touched his arm.

"How about a bourbon, Zeb?"

He shook his head. "No. No thank you," he said, finally taking his eyes from Jennifer and seating himself.

Soup was served, and Bella answered Max and Jolene's inquiries about her home and town. Zeb heard little of it. He could not stop himself from looking across the table, and she returned his regard but made no movement other than to sip her wine and nod to Max or Jolene. Dishes were cleared and Zeb stood abruptly, bringing a servant forward to catch his chair. He walked around the table, oblivious to the now awkward silence filling the room.

"May I speak to you, Miss Crawford?" he said when he stopped beside her chair, napkin still in his hand.

She nodded. "Please do."

"Perhaps I can call on you tomorrow. We could take a drive through the city or a walk if the weather is amenable."

"If you wish," she whispered as she glanced around the table.

It was then that Zeb realized what he'd done. Max was staring at him, elbows on the table, hands folded together as if in prayer. Jolene was looking at the wineglass she was picking up with pursed lips and raised brows.

"Zebidiah?" Bella said. "The main course is being served. Perhaps you can pour me a sherry."

* * *

Jennifer's hands stopped shaking and she felt confident enough to pick up her wineglass and bring it to her lips. She laughed at a silly comment Jolene made and even asked Bella Moran a question. She meant to avoid looking at him, at Zeb, but couldn't stop herself. He still was everything true and right. He was her hero and savior and still as handsome as could be, his blond-brown hair a little longer than usual. He was still broad shouldered with an angled, masculine face, now looking at her with his water blue eyes.

She had missed him so! Yet when they adjourned to the parlor for desserts and coffee, she seated herself beside Max on a settee, leaving no room for Zeb to be near her. When he and his sister rose to leave, he walked to her and sat on a hassock nearby.

"Would the afternoon be convenient for you to step out with me tomorrow? Maybe we can visit a museum or a shop?"

"Perhaps your sister would like to join us," she said.

"Certainly," he said, and looked at Bella.

"I'm sorry to spoil your plans, but Bella and I have already arranged to visit the theatre tomorrow. Isn't that right, Bella?" Jolene asked.

"Yes. Yes. We have already made plans," Bella said. "I'm sorry Zebidiah. I won't be able to join your party. Another day, perhaps?"

"Yes. We will all go another day. It will just be Miss Crawford and I tomorrow if that is agreeable to her."

Jennifer thought Zeb looked triumphant with his response. He rose, eyes on her, finally turning to leave, when his sister prompted him to do so. Jennifer happily wished that the floor would open up and she be swallowed up in nothingness and quietly leave with the memories of all those who were dear to her. But wasn't that exactly what Mrs. Jenners had spoken to her about? Why should she slip away? She had survived!

Max kissed Jolene's cheek and patted Jennifer's hand when she held it out to him. "I'm exhausted. If you ladies don't mind, I'd like to relax and do some reading in my study before retiring. I'll check in on Melinda and Andrew before I go to bed."

"I'm going to sit up a bit. Jennifer? Will you join me? I could have coffee and desserts brought to my sitting room where there are two cozy chairs for a pair of sisters who have not seen each other in ages to curl up in and gab!" Jolene said.

She shook her head. "I'm very tired, Jolene. Perhaps another night?"

"Oh. Of course. How thoughtless I'm being. Traveling can be quite exhausting."

Jennifer knew her sister was disappointed. She'd said earlier, shortly after Jennifer had arrived, how much she had missed her and was looking forward to talking to her. What a coward she was! But she wasn't one really, was she? And what was she scared of? The same things that had kept her sleepless for the last half year.

They climbed the marble steps together, and when Jolene was about to enter her bedroom, Jennifer called out. "Wait. Tea and a cake sound good, and I can sleep late tomorrow."

Jolene walked to her smiling. "Are you sure? I know your trip was arduous."

"I slept a bit before dinner. I'm fine. Really. I intend to do nothing more than stare at your newest child on this visit. Andrew is already quite handsome."

"He takes after his father in looks and is a sweet child. I'm so glad you are here to meet him," Jolene said just as a maid came on to the landing. "Please have Mrs. Trundle send our desserts and a drink cart to my sitting room."

Jennifer followed Jolene to her rooms and slipped off her shoes, digging her toes in the soft carpet under her feet. A maid knocked and rolled in a cart of pastries and a steaming pot of tea. Jennifer pulled her feet under her and stared into the fire.

"Zebidiah Moran is still taken with you, I saw this evening," Jolene said when they were alone. "He is a good man."

"He is the best of men," she replied. "I would not be sitting here if it were not for him."

"He acted as though he hadn't seen or talked to you since . . . since . . . for quite some time. I thought Maximillian told me he had traveled to Boston a few months ago."

"I haven't seen him since the night of the Hospital Soiree. Although I believe he did visit Boston in the early part of the summer."

"And he did not stop at Willow Tree? I can hardly believe it!"

"He did call on us," Jennifer said, and stood to prepare a cup of tea.

"I imagine he was just as attentive then as he was tonight. Smitten, I'd say," Jolene said and accepted a cup of tea.

"I really don't know. He visited with Father."

Jolene turned in her chair. "Are you saying you didn't see him while he was there? In Boston? At Willow Tree?"

Jennifer shook her head. "Mother was indisposed, and I wasn't up to callers as of yet."

"Really? I thought you had begun your work at the bank by then. That's at least what I thought your and Father's letters said, but perhaps I was mistaken. Has he written you?"

Jennifer sat very still, listening to the crackle of the fire and the clink of the silver spoon against bone china as she stirred a sugar cube in her tea. There was very little reason to lie, no reason at all actually. She thought about what Mrs. Jenners had said to O'Brien just last week. Speech is freeing, she said. Even troubling truths are better said aloud than buried.

"I was back to work at the bank by then, although O'Brien was not. She just recently began to go with me. I will be curious to see if she goes by herself this week."

"Will you tell me why you didn't visit with Zebidiah when he was in Boston? Mother may have been indisposed, when isn't she, but you were taking callers if you'd already begun to go back to the bank. Was it something he'd done?"

"I could not bring myself to face him. I couldn't do it. I was mortified! I still am," Jennifer said in a rush.

"Mortified? I don't understand."

Jennifer shrugged, feeling her neck and ears redden with embarrassment. "I defied everything that everyone told me, leaving him to risk everything to save me, and for him to see me there." She closed her eyes, instantly envisioning that night, that hallway, the smells and the sounds.

Jolene knelt in front of her. "Jennifer. You mustn't be embarrassed. There is nothing you could have done differently. Mother and that . . . that man had it planned."

Jennifer leaned forward, close to her sister's face, her eyes filling with tears. "Even when Zeb saw me on the floor, with no skirts, knowing full well what Rothchild intended?"

"No. I will not let you think of yourself as if you did anything wrong," Jolene said and grabbed her hands. "This is not your fault."

"It *isn't* my fault. I have been speaking to a woman who comes and visits O'Brien. I have actually been doing very well. My nightmares are rare and I am able to be alone outside of my rooms. But Zeb is different. I don't think I'll ever be comfortable with him again! How can I be? I respected and cared for him and he was witness to my humiliation!"

"Jennifer, dear," Jolene said, a tear at the corner of her eye. "Do you realize how very glad we are, he is, that you are alive? That you faced this monster and were the victor? When I think of you having to defend yourself with a knife . . . it is too much to think about. You are brave beyond words."

Jennifer kissed her cheek. "It means the world to me that you think so."

Jolene reseated herself and swiped at her eyes. "You must tell me about the woman who visits O'Brien."

"Mrs. Jenners? She is a woman who attends church with Mr. O'Brien. She has spoken to other women when they've encountered violence. She comes and talks to O'Brien and me. She has set me free."

"Has she been a victim of violence herself?"

Jennifer closed her eyes. "Of a level you cannot imagine. Her arms are covered with burns from a cigar and she has a terrible limp. Her leg was broken and never set properly when her husband beat her."

Jolene shook her head. "I hope her tormentor is gone."

"He is. He was drunk as he usually was and walking on the edge of the dock. He lost his balance and fell in. It was storming and the seas were high and strong. No one went in after him, thank the dear Lord."

"And she speaks to others about this?"

"Yes. There is something about her. Something soothing and restful that lures me to speak openly and when I do, I inevitably feel better, even if it takes days or weeks to digest what she has said. For months I woke with terrible pain in my feet, long after all the cuts had healed over. I would wake in a cold sweat, screaming sometimes, feeling as though someone was stabbing me in the sole of my foot."

"What . . . did something . . . I did not know that your feet had been cut. When I was there at Willow Tree you were mostly abed and I did not stay long. What happened?"

"Of course you did not. You were in a delicate condition. I was amazed that Max let you make the journey."

"What happened, Jennifer?"

Jennifer stared away, not willing to look at her sister's face. "When he told me what he was going to do to me, I ran into a dark room, praying it was the kitchen. It was. I'd lost one slipper when he dragged me up the outside steps and when I swept my arm over the counter I knocked china and glasses to the floor. I was standing there in one shoe, going back and forth from foot to foot in my fear and stepping on shards of glass and crockery. I had no idea I'd done it until I woke up and Dr. Roderdeck was pulling glass from my feet."

Jolene covered her mouth with one hand. "My God," she said and shook her head. "You may tell me anything you need to tell me or tell me nothing at all, Jennifer."

"I am tired now," Jennifer said as she stood. "You asked me earlier if Zeb and I had corresponded. He wrote me many letters until I returned them all to him and asked him to not send any more. How I regret that I stopped him! Some days I lived for his letter, as it felt as if it were the only thing keeping me from losing my mind. I had nearly memorized them I'd read them so often."

"You never wrote back?"

"Just the once, asking him to not send any more."

"But, why?"

"I'm not sure. But I've come to talk to him now. Perhaps we can correspond again."

"Oh, darling. Don't let time, or anger, or fears keep you from what is precious like I did. Let him into your heart. He has not been himself for missing you."

"Good night, Jolene. I am glad I am here to meet Andrew and see you and Max and Melinda. I was happy to meet Bella, too. I was very, very glad to see Zeb with my own eyes, and touch his hand when we parted. Be assured, I'm determined to be happy. I will not have that man win from the grave."

* * *

Zeb straightened his hair, hat in hand as he stood on the doorstep of Max and Jolene's home the following day, Bella by his side. He'd been so shocked to see Jennifer last night that he'd acted like a fool, like a young buck with no self-control rather than the chief of staff to an important U. S. senator, writing law and bills for consideration at the Capitol. But the sight of her . . . it did things to him. Things that no woman before, or ever, did to him. He was happy as the next man to view a beautiful woman, to speak with a lively, intelligent one and be pleased. But this was not just an appreciation of the senses, of sight and sound and fragrance. She encompassed all those things and connections unseen as well, where only instinct guides a heart. The only thing left to do was to convince her of that, to remain steadfast and let her know what she meant to him with his words and deeds.

Zeb waited as the housekeeper sent word abovestairs that they'd arrived. Within minutes, Jennifer and Jolene came down the steps and exchanged pleasantries. Jolene took his sister by the arm and climbed in the Shelby carriage. They waved merrily and drove away, leaving Jennifer and him alone and silent.

It hit him in that moment that he was happy, in her company, to be near her or speak to her, especially to kiss her. He smiled at her.

"Would you like to take a walk? Or we can take a ride in my carriage? What would you like to do?"

"Either would be fine, but it is a bit warm for September. The breeze on a carriage ride would be pleasant."

"A carriage ride it is then," he said, helping her into her seat and touching her hand as he did, eliciting a glance in his direction.

"It is wonderful to be back visiting Jolene and Max. I've missed Melinda and have spent the morning in company with my new nephew, Andrew," Jennifer said as she looked around at the buildings they passed on the streets.

"I've been fortunate to be invited often to their home and have maintained a relationship with Melinda. She is dear to me. I live close by and sometimes show up when I know dinner is about to be served."

She laughed. "Where do you live, Zeb? Are we close by? I often think of the story you told about Jolene finding you a house and spending quite a bit to furnish it."

"The bills were a shock but she was right. I needed an address in a good neighborhood, with staff to help me," he said. "There it is up ahead. With the white shutters and the white door."

"How lovely," she said as the carriage slowed, and turned to look at him. "May I see the inside?"

"Yes, of course. Smithers is there and my housekeeper as well to act as chaperones," he said and came around the carriage to hand her down. "Are you sure you're comfortable? Being alone with me? When you sent back my letters, I assumed you . . . I don't know what I assumed, only that you didn't want to see me again. I was very happy you agreed to spend some time with me today but I would never presume—"

Jennifer stopped him with a finger to her lips. "I'd like to talk to you, but I'd rather not do it publically or when there is a possibility of interruption. May we go in?"

Zeb led her inside and handed his hat off to Smithers. "Please," he said as he opened a door at the back of the wide hallway. "This is my study, and there are two comfortable chairs near the window, courtesy of your sister."

They sat in companionable silence, looking out the window at the shrubbery and late-blooming flowers in the small garden behind his house, until she turned in her seat to him.

"Um, I must . . . tell me about what you do for Max."

He looked at her, at a loss as to why she might be interested in his work when he'd hoped they'd be able to speak about more personal issues, but he would indulge and comfort her in any way he could. "I write bills and proposals for laws, according to what Max is thinking in that subject's regard. I make sure we have enough staff to do the research and keep up with correspondence. I befriend my counterparts working for other senators when we need votes." He paused, then continued with a more detailed description as she encouraged him to go on. Her face was pasty white, he noticed then, and she was rubbing her hands together in an unconscious motion. "I make sure that—"

"He said I was a whore. He said he was going to make me bend over a kitchen chair," she said then in a rush, tears suddenly streaming down her face.

Zeb stood abruptly, holding his hands behind his back and doing everything he could do to keep from putting his fist through the pane of glass ahead, or throwing the delicate Chinese vase across the room and reveling in the crash it would make when it hit the brick hearth of the fireplace. He took some deep, calming breaths and looked at Jennifer. Her shoulders were shaking. She looked up at him, and her look of misery was more devastating than anything he'd ever heard or witnessed. He was in physical pain seeing the look on her face, knowing that his agony was nothing compared to hers.

"I am soiled somehow, as if he had used me when he didn't. I've felt I'm not worthy of your notice," she said through trembling lips. "I've never told anyone all the things he said. I couldn't bear to repeat them. I couldn't imagine what someone would think, I only knew that if I'd heard someone else describe the same things I'd be repulsed. Even knowing the person saying it was not the guilty party."

"And is that why you returned my letters?" he asked and knelt on one knee before her. He longed to embrace her, hold her until she felt safe and secure, but he sensed that what she was saying was the reason she was seeing him at all. That she had to say her piece. He would let her fight her way through what she must. It was, perhaps, the only way she could be free.

She nodded. "I was not able to face you before today, did not know if I would be able to even yet. I read your letters time and again and they reminded me of that night, of what you'd seen and thought. But I want you to know they kept me sane when I truly thought I might be losing my mind during those dreary weeks."

Zeb looked at her then until she met his gaze. "Tell me everything he said. Tell me every detail."

Tears spilled down Jennifer's face, and she nodded. She put her hands on his shoulders to pull him close and whispered into his ear every sordid word that had plagued her over the last six months. She spoke softly, without emotion, so close to him that his hair touched her face, and her eyes focused on the golden strands and nothing else. She could feel his muscles contract and tense under her fingers on his shoulder but he did not move or lift his hands from where they lay across his thigh to touch her. She would be forever grateful to him for allowing her to say the words that had haunted her, and by doing so, maybe lessen their hold on her psyche.

Those words, the ugly words, that Rothchild and her own mother had said had reverberated in her head these long months, clattering from one side of her mind to the other, like the clapper in a massive bell. There was silence now as she finished, quietly sobbing with the release. She sat up and looked at him. She did not see pity, which she was glad of. He picked up her hands and kissed the back of each one.

"You do know that you were not the one to say those things or even think them. He was the villain, perhaps out of his mind, not that I care as long as he is dead and gone from our lives. But he was the one to say these words. Not you."

"I do know that, but after that night, I felt as if somehow I deserved his torment even knowing in my mind that I am a good person and that no one deserves that sort of treatment. But that does not stop how I *feel*."

"No one should have to go through what you have been through. I admire you more than I can convey. There is little doubt that I love you," he said, and looked at her with resolve. "I love you. I am the one that is not worthy of *you*. How could I be in the face of your courage and stoicism?"

She kissed him them. Kissed him liked she had dreamed of doing when she could hold the demons at bay. His shaking hands captured her face. "This is the only place in the world that I feel completely safe."

Zeb pulled her to her feet then, and pressed her to him, her breasts against his chest and her legs entwined with his. He wrapped an arm around her back and touched the back of her head with the other, pulling her lips to his until they touched, and his eyes closed. Jennifer kept her eyes open at first, confirming a moment at a time that this was Zebidiah, the man who loved her and honored her and admired her. But there were no ghosts threatening her consciousness, no fear, only complete trust in the man kissing her.

His tongue licked the seam of her mouth, touching her tongue when her lips parted. She felt his face with her fingertips, clean-shaven and smooth, smelling his scent and loving the way she felt in his arms, feminine and alluring when he pulled her hips to his, leaving no doubt of his physical need for her. His eyes were open now, staring at her from under hooded brows, as he ran a finger down her neck to her cleavage, grazing her breast with the back of his hand. She groaned when he touched her so intimately.

Jennifer closed her eyes and ran her hands over his shoulders, down his arms, finally touching his chest, all solid muscle, pulsing with heat. She let her hand drift lower, testing herself, answering the questions that she'd tortured herself with for months. She touched him then, his sex, through his pants, feeling the long, stiff outline on her palm, and was not repulsed or frightened as she'd worried she might be, but rather emboldened as he drew in short breaths through clenched teeth. Her breasts were heavy and her lower insides thrummed with anticipation and heat.

"Jenny," he whispered and covered her hand with his.

A knock at the door sent them jumping apart, she straightening her hair and he buttoning his long suit jacket.

Smithers popped his head through the door. "Will Miss Crawford be staying for dinner, sir?"

"Please don't trouble yourself, Smithers," she said. "We'll be going soon, but I am looking forward to returning."

Smithers nodded with a smile and closed the door. Jennifer turned to Zeb and covered her mouth with her fingers. "That was very close, was it not?" she said with the slightest grin.

"It was very close," he said and took her hands in his. "I cannot describe to you how happy I feel when I see you smile. You are beautiful beyond words."

She smiled up at him. "I think I should go back to Jolene's. Will you be joining us for dinner?"

Chapter Fifteen

"TELL ME ABOUT YOUR WORK at the Crawford Bank, Jennifer?" Max asked as he cut his beefsteak.

"Let my sister eat before you begin your interrogation," Jolene said and looked at Jennifer as they ate dinner the following evening. "He has been asking me all sorts of questions about what I did at the bank and what you do at the bank. I told him I was little more than a hostess but I believe you had much more demanding duties."

"Originally, I did exactly what you had always done, and Father was none too happy as I was still unmarried. I convinced him, though, that it was unexceptional with

O'Brien as an escort, and then one day he brought an account packet to me that the bank's bookkeepers were having difficulty balancing. After that, O'Brien and I began doing that sort of work on a regular basis."

"You had the best marks of any of us at Ramsey, especially in mathematics," Jolene said and looked at Zeb. "My sister is exceptionally bright lest you forget that."

Jennifer's face colored with the praise, even more so as he continued to stare at her admiringly. "I don't intend to forget."

Max chuckled. "How did it occur to you that Rothchild was dipping his fingers into company funds?"

The room was silent then, all eyes on Jennifer's ashen face. It took Max a moment to realize she was not answering and that his wife was staring daggers at him.

"Why don't we spend tomorrow afternoon shopping, Jennifer? Perhaps Bella would like to join us," Jolene said hurriedly. "I need at least three new hats and shoes to match some dresses that have recently arrived."

Zeb watched Jennifer. She was doing her best to remain calm, and even looked up at Max with a tentative smile. He did not believe she'd said Rothchild's name since the night of the Hospital Soiree. She looked at him, and he watched her shoulders rise and fall with a deep breath. He hoped it was possible to will another person encouragement because that was what he was trying to do with his look to her.

"Mr. Rothchild," she said and paused. "Adjusted the percentages the bank charged on a loan, on a particular piece of collateral, and then hid the difference in the credit and debit columns. His assistant, Mr. Jefferson, did cash tallies and pocketed the overage."

"How did you ever discover it?" Jolene asked.

"It was a mystery to me and O'Brien but we found patterns in multiple accounts and were able to follow the amounts."

"And you are back to work now?" Max asked.

"I am. I was not convinced I would ever be able to return but I have, and my father has turned over some significant projects to me. It has been very challenging but also very rewarding."

"Why am I not surprised that you, the quietest of the three of us, are leading the way at the bank? You will be the president when Father retires. And I for one couldn't be happier that you will be leading our family business into the next century. Perhaps Melinda would like to spend some time with you there after she is through her education. I think a toast is in order," Jolene said, and raised her wineglass.

"Hear, hear," Max said with a broad smile. "To Jennifer Crawford."

It suddenly occurred to Zeb that Jennifer would not be leaving Boston anytime soon. His plan to ask her to marry him was now in question. How would he honor his commitment to Max and be in the same state as his intended bride? Then he looked at her, at her shy, proud smile, accepting the good wishes of her sister and brother-in-law. It would not matter where they lived, he supposed. He was in love with her and would find useful work wherever she was and Max would have to find a new chief of staff.

"To my extraordinary younger sister. I wish you all the happiness that I have found," Jolene said.

"To the smartest, bravest, most beautiful banker Boston has ever seen," Zeb said and met her eyes.

* * *

"Where shall we go today?" Zeb asked her as moved his carriage out into the traffic of the street. "A park? A museum? Shopping? I am at your service."

Jennifer looked at him, at his strong profile, and watched his hands work the reins. He was the dearest of men, and she was feeling better about herself than she had in ages. It was easier to smile and laugh, and all the horrifying images she'd harbored, including the sight of Jeffrey Rothchild's face as he gurgled his last breath, had faded to some degree in her consciousness. Not that she could not conjure them up if she tried, but why try? Why not reach for happiness and normalcy? And there were things that needed to be said between them. Things she did not remember or know that only he could supply and other things she'd never shared with him. It was time. Time for one less burden.

"I'd like to go to your house again, Zeb," she said.

He turned the carriage onto his street and handed off the reins to the all-about boy. Zeb showed her in to his study and ordered coffee and cookies.

"Are you missing work today?" she asked.

"Not really," Zeb said as he sat down in the chair beside her. "Somedays I work eighteen hours a day and do so seven days a week. It is relatively quiet now as the Senate is not in session, but Max has always told me to take whatever time I can. So I am."

Jennifer sat quietly, thinking about what to say, what questions to ask, when Zeb took her hand in his, and rubbed slow circles on her palm. She relaxed and leaned her head back against the cushion, thinking about all the unanswered questions for them both.

"I thought about exposing Mother's duplicity with Jeffrey. I ached to shout it out, that my mother was a horrible person, willing to sacrifice her daughter for her own selfishness. In the end, I could not do it."

"I have wondered what happened between you and your mother and father. I hoped for your sake that you would be able to come to terms with whatever it was."

"My mother has recovered from her surgery but her mental state is in a decline. She sometimes calls me Julia or Jolene or Mildred, her maid that father dismissed. She rarely comes out of her rooms and we have hired a nurse to be with her during the day. Her new maid spends the evenings with her and sleeps in her dressing room. I usually spell her for an hour or two in the evening and read aloud," she said and looked at him. "When it was all said and done, I could not hate her."

"I am sorry to say I am not so forgiving."

"You should have seen my father's face when it was all finally revealed to him," Jennifer said and squeezed his hand. "He marched to Mother's bedroom and slammed the door behind him after he had dismissed her maid. I could hear his shouting from my bedroom. I could not stop crying. I felt like I had torn my family apart."

"You have held your family together."

"I have in some ways. Father and I are on good terms and dine together every evening. He is very protective of me now. It is a stark dichotomy to his absentmindedness that I have lived with all of my life. He has lost all regard for Mother. He is a dutiful caretaker, making sure the staff manages her respectfully and kindly; however, he never visits her now."

"She put you in danger. She is your mother and always will be, but I cannot have your forbearance. I can't pretend to feel any way other than how I do."

"I don't expect you to," she said. "What happened when you arrived in Boston? I have only been able to piece together what I have heard when Father or Jolene or O'Brien did not know I was awake."

"What a horrible day," he said softly and told her about the delayed train and Hadley giving him directions with O'Brien's help. "There was a woman on that street who heard you shouting. She said you looked directly at her. Do you remember?"

Jennifer nodded, feeling far away from Zeb's comfortable chair in Washington. "She was standing on her stoop. I screamed for her to help me but Rothchild covered my mouth, and when I bit his hand, he slapped me. I was dazed and terrified."

"I would gladly kill him again for hitting you."

Filmy images from that night played in front of her eyes. She squeezed Zeb's hand, her link to the current world, and took in a long, slow breath as she saw herself desperately grabbing for a weapon, cutting her thumb on the blade when she found it. Then Zeb was there. Flying through the wooden door to her rescue, and she feeling as though she could no longer stand on her two legs. "And you shot him. I had not killed him?"

"He followed you into the hallway and his arm was raised above you, holding a bloody knife. I shot him just as he meant to stab you with it," Zeb said and turned in his seat to face her. "I have no regrets."

"Nor I. Did the police come?"

He nodded. "I spent several days at the station answering questions. Hadley and O'Brien followed me to Jefferson's house that night and knew I'd gone to the station house. I was able to get word to Jolene through them of my whereabouts. I did not want you to think I'd deserted you."

"Why did the police hold you? Surely they knew about my injuries."

"Most likely because I wouldn't say a word to them. They didn't know if I was the perpetrator or the defender."

Jennifer shook her head. "But why? Why not just tell them everything?"

"It wasn't my story to tell. You were concerned about the bank, about your family. I was not going to say anything that might cause you distress. Eventually they spoke to the woman who heard you shouting, and then your father came."

"Father?"

"He told them everything. I asked him if he was concerned about the bank's reputation and he said very clearly, 'The bank be damned.'"

"I had no idea. I was too terrified to leave my bed for days. When there was a loud noise from the street or the kitchens, I hid in my dressing room, and then someone would get O'Brien and she would coax me into bed and sit with me until I slept."

"She has been a good friend."

"She has. It's strange, how one's emotions can overtake reason. I knew he was dead. I watched him die but every time someone knocked on my bedroom door, I thought it was him. My mind played tricks on me."

"But you are healing. I can see that."

"I am. I am much better for seeing and talking to you. You are far too kind."

"No. There is no such thing as too kind," he said and sat forward, elbows on his knees, staring out the window.

"And I'm in love with you. Do not feel any obligation to reciprocate. My love is freely given to you without expectation," he said with a quick glance over his shoulder.

"But I denied your advice, wise advice, and put you and others in danger. I did not listen to my sister or even my own good sense. I worry I am not worthy of any regard. This mess was of my own making."

"I forgive you," he said with a smile as he stood and offered her his hand. "Come. Let us go to a park or a shop or somewhere we are not concentrating on grim times. We are alive and well. Our troubles are behind us, and we have both learned something about ourselves."

Jennifer laid her hand in his and looked up at him. "I *have* learned something. Something momentous." His image shimmered before her and she smiled. "I have learned to listen to my own heart and follow my own sense. I hear it speaking to me now."

"What is it saying to you?" he whispered and pulled her to her feet.

"It is saying that you are the man of my dreams. The one who will keep me safe in the harbor of your arms and love me even at my worst and my weakest. It is saying you are the most honorable man of my acquaintance. The type of man who I would want to build a life with. It is saying I love you."

Zeb pulled her close, flush against him, with one arm around her waist and one on the nape of her neck. Holding her still and tight with a fierceness she'd never seen from him. He stared at her lips and then claimed them, roughly impatient and tender in the same stroke. He growled and ran his hand down her back and pulled her bottom tight against him. He broke the kiss and touched his forehead to hers.

"Put me out of my lovesick misery and marry me. Please."

"Yes," she said, and nodded. "Yes. I will marry you."

* * *

Jennifer was not certain if she would ever become accustomed to watching her husband wander around their bedroom without a stitch of clothing on. Not that she did not love looking at him; she did. He was broad shouldered and all long, lean, corded arms attached to a chest with a line of horizontal shadow for each rippling muscle. Long legs, now walking toward her. He had said a resounding, clear, and loud "no" when she'd suggested early after their wedding that many married couples had separate bedrooms and dressing rooms.

"What are you thinking about, darling?"

"That you have not a drip of shame in your veins," she said, and undid the bow of her robe, pulling it off and hanging it over the bedpost.

"And why should I," he said as he jumped on the mattress, pulling her down beside him and capturing her legs with his and snuggling her ear. "We are in the privacy of our own room. We are married adults."

She watched as his eyes hooded and he followed his finger as it made a slow descent down her neck and to her breast, stopping just shy of its peak. He looked at her then in the way he did that made her breath come in gasps and her body ache to be covered with his. She was a wanton in his arms, she admitted, and there was nothing in her history or experience to compare to how she felt when she was with Zebidiah in their bed. There was a carnal need that she'd never felt before, and while she was glad that their wedding night had been in a room with only candlelight as they'd touched each other with trembling hands, she was equally glad to know that their mutual sexuality brought her comfort with no fear or shame, and that the more she experienced with her husband, and he with her, the more ravenous and knowing they were with each other.

Jennifer reached up and pushed his hair from his face. "You are so very handsome."

"I know you're beautiful, but there are some parts you're hiding with this silky nightie. Let me help you take it off," he said as she sat upright beside him.

Zeb pulled the silk nightgown over her head, leaving her bare. She resisted the urge to cover herself with the sheets as he stared at her and hissed between his teeth. He lifted her breast in his hand, kneading her and touching her nipple with his thumb. She steadied herself on her arms behind her and watched him make slow circles, not touching her anywhere but where his palm held the weight of her breast.

She touched her lip with her tongue, and watched his sex harden. She leaned down and kissed him then, there, on the tip of his cock, running her tongue around the ridge. He dropped back on the mattress with a shudder and groaned. What power she had! She licked the length of him and watched his chest rise and fall, finally taking him in her mouth slowly.

"Come here," he whispered. "Please."

She climbed atop him, already warm and pulsing between her legs. She sat up on her knees, her hands on his shoulders, as he rubbed the head of his sex against her until she was moaning and wet and gyrating against him.

"Please," she said.

Zeb entered her with one, long, smooth motion, bringing a cry from them both. He worked in her, holding her hips still, as their eyes met, half-lidded and far gone in sexual passion. Jennifer dropped onto his chest, her breasts against his hot, wet skin. She felt the spasm of his last thrust and heard a grating cry from his chest. He shook a final tremor, and she stretched out on him languidly, unable to summon her limbs to move.

He rolled her onto her back, looming over her and touching her face softly with his fingertips. "I love you, Jenny. I always will."

"I love you, Zebidiah. With every bit of myself, until we are old and infirm. Until the only thing left is love."

Epilogue

Boston 1894

HOW SAD FATHER LOOKS," JULIA said. "He has barely eaten all day."

Jolene lifted Andrew onto her lap and kissed his forehead. "He is sad. Not matter what she had done, no matter how angry or disappointed he was with her, he still loved her. Desperately."

"It has been a long, unpleasant time for the last few months until she passed on," Jennifer said.

"It is still very difficult for me to feel any sympathy for her, even in her suffering," Julia said and dabbed at her eyes. "But I still feel terribly guilty that I did not visit her before she died."

Jolene, Julia, and Jennifer, the Crawford sisters, sat together at a table in the vast ballroom of Willow Tree set up for hundreds of mourners to dine on the day of Jane Crawford's funeral. Guests were still trickling in the door, although their father had said he would continue to greet late arrivals and that they should spend their time together.

"Guilt is not productive, I've found," Jolene said, and handed Andrew off to his nanny. "Don't indulge yourself, Julia, past a few days of moping. Our mother was never a happy woman, devious in her prime and dangerous as she was slowly swallowed up by her mental incapacities. But our past does not define our future."

"True. Look at us," Julia said and squeezed Jolene's hand. "We have all been tested by some degree of fire and come out the victor, but more importantly we have found love."

Jennifer turned her head to gaze in the direction that her sisters looked. Their husbands stood together as a group, Jake with Mary Lou on his shoulders and Jillian and Jacob by his side, and Max taking little Andrew from the nanny's arms and tossing him in the air. She could hear his baby giggles from where she sat. Zeb smiled and watched Andrew, up and down, up and down, his arm around Melinda's shoulders.

"What do you think Father will do, Jennifer, now that Mother is gone? Will he stay here and rattle around this massive house alone? Are you and Zeb going to live with him?" Julia asked.

"We discussed that but neither of us wants to live here, in this grand of a house. We have recently spoken to Father about moving somewhere smaller or with us when Zeb and I find a home," she replied.

"Maximillian gives Zebidiah unheralded credit for living under the same roof as Mother," Jolene said. "I told him he did it for you."

"He did. He didn't like the idea at all and on the rare occasion he needed to find me when I was helping Mother eat or reading to her, he would be angry at the sight of her. She called him Jeffrey once."

Julia covered her mouth with her hand and Jolene's eyes widened.

"You may laugh if you wish. I did when he met me in our bedroom later."

"I would never laugh," Julia said and touched her hand. "Knowing how evil and horrible that man was. How you barely escaped and how grateful I am and was. I prayed every night for you after I got Jolene's letters."

Jennifer shrugged and smiled. "There was certainly nothing humorous about my dealings with Rothchild, but you must admit Mother thinking that Zeb was he, and calling out to him that evening, was, if not funny then certainly ironic."

Jolene leaned forward in her seat and covered Jennifer's hand with her own. "You are over it then. You have come to terms with . . . all of it."

"No more or less than you have come to terms with Little William's death, or Julia with being parted from

Jillian all those years. But we battle on, don't we? If we hadn't we would not have found our husbands, the loves of our lives. You two would not have your children and I would not have my nieces and nephews and another addition to our family that will present him or herself in seven months or so," Jennifer said and touched her stomach.

"Congratulations!" Jolene said and leaned forward to kiss her cheek.

"What wonderful news!" Julia cried. "What will the bank do without you?"

"The Crawford Bank will soon have new blood. Zeb will begin working with Father in less than three weeks. He will finally be done traveling back and forth to Washington helping Max get settled with a new chief of staff."

"Perfect," Jolene said. "An honorable man to carry on our family business for the next generation."

"None of it would be possible without these wonderful men in our lives," Julia said. "Your husbands are as dear to me as my own."

"Nor without the strength and courage of the women in this family," Jolene said and held her sister's hands.

Jennifer held Julia's hand then, completing the circle of family, and looked at the two women beside her. "Nor without love. Love does not end, even with tragedy and sadness, and has given us the will to go on."

Hello Readers!

Thank you for purchasing *Her Safe Harbor,* Crawford Family Book 4. I hope you enjoyed Zeb and Jennifer's story. Please share your thoughts with friends and family and with others on review sites and social media. The first book in this series is *Train Station Bride*, the second book is *Contract to Wed*, and *The Maid's Quarters* Crawford Family Book 3, is a novella featuring a character from *Contract to Wed.*

Follow me on Face Book at Holly Bush, at hollybushbooks.com, or on Twitter @hollybushbooks to hear all the latest updates. I love to hear from readers!

You can also read excerpts from my other Prairie Historicals, *Romancing Olive, Reconstructing Jackson,* and Victorian Romances, *Cross the Ocean* and *Charming the Duke* at my website. *Red, White and Screwed*, a Women's Fiction title, is a new category for me and I'm hoping you'll give it a try! Find these books at Amazon, Barnes & Noble, Kobo, and Itunes. Thanks again for your purchase! A sample of *Romancing Olive* is below.

Romancing Olive - Excerpt

Spencer, Ohio 1891

Olive Wilkins found the sheriff's office as promised, beside a busy general store. The walls were thick stone, and the bars at the windows cast striped patterns on the floor. A weary-faced man with sun-toughened skin sat behind the desk.

"Just a minute . . ." the sheriff said.

Olive waited dutifully as he wrote, letting her eyes wander from the cells in the corner of the room to the gun belt looped over the hook near the door to the sign proclaiming Sheriff Bentley the law in this small Ohio town.

"What can I help you with, ma'am?' he asked, as he looked up from his papers and tilted back his hat.

"My name is Olive Wilkins, and my brother, James Wilkins, and his wife, Sophie, lived here in Spencer. I am here to take his children back to my home in Philadelphia, but I am not quite sure with whom they are staying. The note from my sister-in-law's family is unclear," Olive explained as she pulled the oft-folded and unfolded letter from her bag.

The sheriff sat back in his chair and tapped his pencil stub against his mouth. "John and Mary are staying with Jacob Butler."

"How are the Butlers related to my brother's wife?"

"They're not," Sheriff Bentley replied.

"Then how did the children come to——"

"None of Sophie's family, the Davises, would take them in," he interrupted.

"Oh."

"Jacob Butler couldn't abide two children living on their own in that shack, so he took them home. He was your brother's closest neighbor," the sheriff explained.

"Sophie's family abandoned them?" Olive asked. Could this man be talking about James's nearest relatives? Could there be two sets of orphaned children in one small community? With the same names? No, there could not be.

"The Davis clan couldn't tell you how many children or dogs belong to them, but they sure didn't want more."

Olive frowned, certain she had misunderstood. "My brother's children lived alone on a farm? Surely Sophie's family would have never ——"

"I don't rightly know I'd call Jimmy's place a farm," the sheriff interjected, and met Olive's bewildered eyes. "The worst part is I don't know how long the children were in the house with their mother dead and if they saw her murder."

Olive's knees threatened to buckle, and her eyes darted from the sheriff's face to her handbag to the desk. "How could that be? The Davises' letter only said that James and Sophie had died. I . . . I just assumed that it had been influenza or a dreadful accident of some kind."

The sheriff stood, came around the desk, and seated Olive in a chair. "Jimmy was killed when he got caught cheating at cards. He wagered the farm, and the man who killed him rode out and tried to stake his claim." He looked away and grimaced. "When I got back to town a couple of days later, I rode out to check on Sophie. It looked like she put up a hell of a fight."

Olive clutched the letter from her brother's in-laws in her hand. In her mind's eye she pictured her only sibling as a young man when she had last seen him. The pride of her mother and father, a charming and handsome boy who filled their Church Street home with laughter. At twenty years of age, he had loved Sophie Davis with such abandon; he'd left all he'd known behind to make a life with his new wife on the plains of Ohio. Sophie's kin were farmers, and she wanted no life other than that which the soil and the tilling of it brought. So James announced his intentions of making Ohio his new home where he would farm and raise his family.

The death of Olive's parents, only a year apart, had left her bereft, but she had cared for them through their illnesses and had seen their demises inch closer with each day. The news of James's and Sophie's deaths, however, left her grief-stricken. But her misery would certainly pale in comparison to the devastation John and Mary must feel. Without preamble, this pair of deaths had orphaned her ten-year-old niece and four-year-old nephew.

"And the children?" Olive asked.

"Couldn't find hide nor hair of them wild things. Searched everywhere. Jacob checked the house about a week later and found them living there. Mary gave him a fight. She was scared to death, even though she knew Jacob and his children. And John, that boy hasn't spoken a word since," he replied.

Tears threatened Olive's eyes. She could not decide which of all of this horrifying news was the worst. *But it could not be.* The sheriff must have some of this information wrong, otherwise . . . "I'll have to make sure that Mr. and Mrs. Butler understand how thankful I am someone took in Mary and John."

The sheriff propped a hip on the corner of his desk. "There is no Mrs. Butler. Jacob's a widower. His wife died a year ago giving birth to their youngest son."

"How . . . can you tell me how to arrange transportation to the Butlers'?" Olive asked.

"I'll be going out that way tomorrow. I'll rent a wagon, unless you ride. No? Then I'll take you out there," he offered.

"That's very kind of you, Sheriff," Olive replied. The social courtesies came without thought while her heart grappled with what the man had said. She pulled her cloak tightly around her and left the office feeling numb.

Olive found herself walking aimlessly through town. In her mind she played and replayed the story the sheriff had told her, and it rubbed raw all that she knew to be true of how she was raised, how James was raised, how life was to be lived. She glanced down and only then realized she still held the letter that had brought the heartbreaking news.

Sophie's family had written her that there was no one to take in the two small children after their parents' deaths, so Olive faced the greatest challenge she had ever known. She would rescue these orphans, blood of her blood, and love them and take them back to Philadelphia where she would raise them in their father's childhood home.

Olive had stared out the train window on the trip to Spencer, mile after mile, dreaming of Sunday afternoons at the ice cream parlor, helping John with his studies, and someday leading Mary into womanhood. What a wonderful continuation of the Wilkinses' legacy Olive would be able to bestow. She would be firm but gentle, patient, with high expectations of these bright shining pennies. She would read them the letters their father had written, take them to church, and love them, and they would love her.

CPSIA information can be obtained
at www.ICGtesting.com
Printed in the USA
BVHW051653220223
659017BV00015B/504

9 781530 269907